THIEF

GO THERE.

OTHER TITLES AVAILABLE FROM PUSH

THIEF

BRIAN JAMES

SCHOLASTIC INC.

NEW YORK   TORONTO   LONDON   AUCKLAND   SYDNEY

MEXICO CITY   NEW DELHI   HONG KONG   BUENOS AIRES

ISBN-13: 978-0-545-03400-5
ISBN-10: 0-545-03400-0

All rights reserved. Published by PUSH, an imprint of Scholastic Inc., 557 Broadway, New York, NY 10012. SCHOLASTIC and associated logos are trademarks and/or registered trademarks of Scholastic Inc.

Library of Congress Cataloging-in-Publication Data
Available

12 11 10 9 8 7 6 5 4 3 2 1   8 9 10 11 12 13/0

Printed in the U.S.A.
First printing, June 2008

For All the Friends Who Have Become My Family

> "I've heard of pious men and I've
> heard of dirty fiends,
> But you don't often hear of us
> ones in between."
>
> —Spencer Krug

AN INVISIBLE INVASION

Seems like someone's always watching me . . around every corner on every city block . . through every crack in the sidewalk . . watching me in the dark and under the covers. Always.

The eyes are empty eyes . . the same as the eyes behind the mask tattooed on my wrist. Blank but watchful.

I pass by them like flashes of color on a movie screen.

They watch me like I'm something beautiful. But they never watch long enough. They turn their back on me too soon . . so they never see my hands slipping into their pockets.

I feel their wallets on my fingertips. I make myself into something too cute for them to ever think I'd steal.

Slip away from them like a tiny dream . . nothing they can remember.

I get away with it every time.

3

Get away through the crowd . . between the people pushed so close together on the subway train . . sliding through them like a ghost changing shapes . . changing sizes . . finding the smallest space to slip through. Brushing against strangers' coats . . against their arms . . the knees of the ones who sit in the seats . . careful never to trip over their feet . . making my way to the door and out at the next stop.

Listen for the computer voice through the speaker.

Stand clear of the closing doors, please.

Obey the warning and I'm on my way . . weaving in and out along the platform and up the stairs . . the beat of my heart like the roll of the train . . fast and getting faster as I pull away.

Coming out of the ground is like making my way back from a grave I never intended to stay in. The flutter of being free.

Dizzy lights of taxi cabs and limousines on the street . . streaks along the avenue like trails from super-heroes leaving messages in fire as they fly.

If I look up at the skyscrapers I'll fall down. There are too many and they're too far away to take in.

Part of me floats up that high . . part of me dancing the way the electricity dances in the windows above the street. I am a tiny ballerina made of light. That's the part of me nobody sees. The rest of me walks like nothing happened on another nothing day.

I have to keep my eyes open for trouble. I have to move carefully. I have to stay invisible.

Cops on every corner lean against walls.

Cops on every street driving in their squad cars.

My ears know the sound of their sirens. I'm trained to run when they call.

There's a clean getaway around every corner as long as I know the way.

Cops can never catch me because the guy I stole the wallet from is a million blocks away by the time he knows. I'm already a part of the background . . a nameless face in an opposite part of the city. He's seen a hundred other people in a hundred other places by then.

I always make sure to look innocent.

Everyone is innocent as long as they get away.

The way I walk is innocent . . sweet with my arms behind my back . . my eyes watching my feet except for a peek up now and then. I keep silent save for a soft sound from my lips . . *la, la, la-la* . . every now and then.

Cute enough to kill . . that's what Alexi calls it. She pets me behind the ear and waits for me to smile for her . . tracing the shape of my mask tattoo with her fingers until I can feel the eyes glow . . letting me touch the one she has that is exactly the same . . on the same wrist . . done with the same pen held under the same lighter.

The mark of a thief.

A black mask over empty eyes.

It's supposed to give us protection . . keep us safe from witnesses. It gives us warning and it gives us more than that. It gives us family.

Ink in our veins like blood we can share.

When we touch them wrist to wrist it makes us sisters.

Sisters and thieves.

There's a cigarette in her hand . . bending slowly to and from her lips as she sits on the steps of the porch.

Her face lights up as she breathes in . . goes dark again when she breathes out . . smoke quickly lost in the shadows off to the side . . fading like the rumble of the train on the platform above our heads.

I can see her bones showing through her skin . . the shape of her cheeks . . at her elbows and knees. Even from this far away I can tell she's fading into nothing.

She told me once that she wanted to be so skinny that she would rot from view.

I told her then that she'd almost made it.

Alive again when she takes another breath . . the dim light from the window behind her like a halo hiding her face. I worry that maybe today will be the one when she actually makes it all the way to becoming invisible.

7

My smile always brings her back.

"You're late," she says when I make myself known . . turning my hips side to side with the song I sing in my head.

Watching the color come back in her face is like watching the first drops of rain roll over the window.

"I lost track of time," I say.

Our words don't mean as much as the way our eyes follow each other. We each make a move to brush our hair away . . mine the color of midnight . . hers more like the white center of the sun.

"How did you make out?" she asks, stepping the cigarette out on the last word. The last spiral of smoke disappears as I reach into my pocket.

My hands are filled with the folded bills from discarded wallets . . wallets left to die in trashcans coming down the subway platform.

I can feel the money's color the way I can feel the green from the stem of a plant between my fingers. "Not too bad, I guess," I say, not knowing the exact amount.

It's never worth counting since I don't keep it. I only care that it's enough to keep Sandra from bitching.

I keep a little for myself, since this time there's plenty. Enough to buy something to eat, maybe. But first I have to make sure Sandra gets the rest.

"A social worker's here . . dropped by just now," Alexi says.

They come once a month . . or at least they're supposed to. It's more like every other month, or less sometimes. It's nothing really . . a few questions . . a quick look around to make sure it's clean . . checklist of food in the kitchen and those kinds of things. Their names never matter . . each of them exactly the same, only with different faces.

I see the shadows in the front room that stretch from the kitchen . . shadows that move their heads in conversation. I can't hear what they're saying. I can only hear the shouting from next door . . the words of the kids gathered under the building security lights across the street . . the roar of cars speeding through the traffic lights . . dogs barking in the tiny caged yards behind each row home.

Alexi glances back to the house and tosses the cigarette filter to the side. Then she waves the smoke from her last breath to keep anyone from seeing.

"Better get in there . . and better keep that away for now," she tells me, motioning my hand back into my pocket with a nod of her head.

I'll have to keep the cash hidden until the social worker leaves . . until I have told my lies and said *please* and *thank you* the way they like me to. I'll smile like the picture inside my case folder, then they can shuffle all their papers in order and put me away safe in a neat stack before they go.

No big trick to it.

I've been in the system long enough . . more than a year, and it's as simple as breathing now. It's not much different than stealing. I act cute and get away with anything.

They keep us all like butterflies. Runaways . . orphans . . any kid without a parent. Scoop us up off the streets as we flutter trying to get away . . sweeping us into a net . . placing us in glass cases in all parts of the city only to pull us out and take a look every once in a while and make sure we're in the same place they left us.

I've been in this same place, with Sandra, for close to a year. Alexi's been here almost three. She taught me all the ways around everything.

They're sitting at the kitchen table when I go in.

Sandra's eyes pass to me in the hallway for a moment, then pass back to the social worker across from her. I can only see the woman's leg . . the worn sole of her red shoes . . the run in her stocking like a wound.

Sandra's eyes are like the puddles that collect on the bottom of the subway tracks . . a green shine like polished ink . . the surface so bright that nothing underneath shows.

"Here's the folder if you just want to take a look," the woman's voice says. Then there's the sound of papers sliding across the plastic table top. "It's just that I'm desperate to find a good home to place him in . . a place like yours where it's stable."

There's a meanness in the way Sandra snaps up the papers only to toss them back down again.

"What do I want with him? We are three girls in this house!" Her accent thicker when she's annoyed. She tells us it's more of a Russian feeling to be angry . . says it brings her back to those places and brings it out in her voice.

I know all about the new kid . . the one Sandra put in for a few weeks ago. "More income," she said. Meaning: another thief and another raise on the check from the city. Alexi turns eighteen this summer and then she'll get to leave. Sandra needs to break in a new thief by then. One who's closer to my age. If he's fifteen she'll get three good years out of him.

"He's a sweet kid," the social worker says.

"No boys."

Boys make terrible thieves.

That's what Sandra's always telling us. She says too many people watch them and no quick smile will make them look away. Nobody falls in love with them just by seeing the way they walk. That's what gives me and Alexi an edge.

I stay in the hallway . . letting myself blend in with the wallpaper . . taking on the pattern until I'm a part of the scenery.

"It's temporary. Only until another place comes available."

It's a trap and I can't help but smile . . putting my hand up to cover my mouth to keep a laugh from getting off my tongue.

Sandra's going to get stuck with this boy. There's no way around it. It's him or nothing. That's the way it works.

Serves her right.

With the way she's always screwing everybody else over, it's about time someone put one over on her.

Her glance comes up from fixing the strap on her blouse. She looks straight at me and her eyes narrow. Her forehead wrinkles as she watches me laugh without a sound.

She gestures for me to come in. Then she says, "Come here for a minute." A sharp look sweeps across her face telling me to make mine blank.

She presents me like she's showing off a new dress. "This is Elizabeth," she tells the social worker, announcing my name like she owns it. Fine with me. Nobody calls me Elizabeth anyway. Everybody just calls me Kid. It fits me better.

"Hi," I say, biting my lip to look shy.

The woman shifts through the folders . . shuffles the one with my name on it to the top and looks up at me . . making sure the photograph matches me . . making sure I'm smiling enough to look healthy.

She's been here before . . but they never remember.

My life is written in the stack of papers under her folded hands . . a list of places that I've stayed . . names of family members . . judges and courthouses . . dates and things like that. Those are the parts about me that don't really exist . . nothing about who I really am . . but they're the only parts they ever care about.

She asks me a few of the simple questions . . ones I only have to nod to and say *yeah* a few times. Then it's back to him . . the boy whose picture sits between them on the table. It's like the photo of every other kid I met when I used to live on the streets. It's the face of a ghost trying to get back to wherever he was before he was born.

"Look," the woman says, her voice stronger now. She leans across the table to make Sandra pay attention. "You want to take in another kid, and he's the one you're going to have to take." She knows the game too. She knows the request Sandra filed is only a request for more money.

A deep breath and a nod of the head is all the answer she needs.

She pushes the chair away from the table and gathers up the folders to put them back in her briefcase.

"I'll bring him by tomorrow evening," she says. The tone of her voice is back to the way it's used to being . . polite . . complimenting . . saying nice things again about how encouraging it is that the kids who come to live with Sandra actually stay.

Alexi walks in as the woman walks out. Then there's the quick spark of a lighter as Sandra breathes in the flames . . breathes out like a dragon.

"That bitch." The syllables slither along the end of her cigarette. She snaps her fingers, and my hand reaches into my pocket. The money is folded every which way when I set it down.

Both of Sandra's hands fall on it like a bird catching prey. She flips through the cash for the highest bills . . trying to forget the battle she just lost.

"We're getting a brother?" Alexi teases. Both of us laugh as curses come like a war storm in another language from Sandra's mouth. The lit end of her cigarette dangles from her lips. Ashes fall with each growl she makes.

RUN AWAY HOME

The sun stays shy . . hiding behind the clouds all day like a little kid hiding behind his mother.

I don't mind though.

Something about the city when it's gray seems to fit . . matching the color of the buildings. The color of the trees this close to winter makes everything feel as safe as being under a blanket.

Strangers' faces go dim on days like this.

Mine lights up.

My feet follow the cobblestones to the river . . past the lonely high rises like glass towers touching the bottom of the sky. At this time of day, all of them are empty like the cars parked along the sidewalk.

Sometimes it feels like every street leads to the same place . . to the same park where I end up so many times.

The benches along the ledge face the river . . looking at

Queens across the way . . empty factories littered among new apartment buildings. If I could see through them and out onto the island, I'd see Sandra's house miles away where the city begins to die and the rest of the world begins.

My bench is empty.

Looks the same as the other ones to the left and to the right . . same length . . same distance from the water . . same chipped green paint . . same everything except that it's mine.

I made this bench my bed once upon a time for two weeks. It knows me when I sit down and let the sound of the river flow through me.

I'm wild in my heart like a wolf . . that's what Sandra says. It's an old legend where she comes from. Girls born like me are children of the wolf . . born with skin the color of snow . . hair the color of midnight . . eyes as wild as the animals in the forest. Born thieves.

"The water calms you like it calms all animals," she tells me.

Only she's wrong about that. There's nothing calm about me when I'm near the river. It feels alive inside me.

My mother used to let me throw wishes into the river. I'd scribble them on tiny pieces of paper and cry as I watched them float away. She'd put her head near my ear . . whisper softly . . tell me how the seagulls would keep my wishes from drowning . . carry them off to the end of the world. One day all the wishes would come back to me on shooting stars.

I wonder where all those scraps of paper ended up. Maybe they're on their way back to me. Maybe they're at the bottom of the river like all the other trash.

Either way I like to sit here and wait . . just watching rust-colored water rush between the little islands. I feel the excitement in me . . beating faster as the wind picks up.

This was my last home on the street . . the last of so many that I can't keep track of them all. Sometimes I pass buildings that I used to stay in. I don't even recognize them with their new paint around new windows . . new walls . . and people actually living in them. Real people paying real rent.

Before it was nobody but homeless kids and rats.

It's all different now . . the city, I mean. It's different from three years ago when I ran for the first time. It's cleaner and bigger. Spreading out and pushing kids like me farther from it.

I was almost dead when they caught me. That's how it always is. They let you waste away in the hidden corners . . wait until you're too weak to run . . pick up your bones like picking up tossed out furniture . . carry you off and set you down somewhere in the middle of their foster care system.

I was lying on this bench when they came for me. I didn't see them . . didn't see anything except the small waves on the water . . letting everything else fade . . letting the river take me away to wherever I was supposed to go next. I was ready to be a ghost.

I remember them like images from a dream . . shadows on the other side of the world I was drifting into. The noise they made broke through like cigarette burns in paper. The crackle of the radio on his belt . . the tap of his wrist against his gun.

"Dispatch we need an ambulance at this location," he said, and I could feel the words as strongly as his hand under my chin. Then nothing for what felt like the longest time.

Two foster homes and twelve court appearances later I ended up in Sandra's care. I've been there almost a year, but it never feels like home. Here is always home . . free and on the run.

Every new part of my life seems to start here by the river.

It must mean something new is starting now if the clouds brought me back . . if the streets all led here like I was following the only path through the maze of the city.

I close my eyes and change my song to something more like the river . . sadder but with something to hope for.

Then I put my face against the wood. The smooth feel of paint is as soft as the feel of Alexi's hand.

Whatever comes next must be good because inside me the sun is shining brighter. Butterfly wings are beginning to show through. And the river is whispering to me . . saying wishes are still being turned into stars all the way at the end of the world.

And I guess if that's true I can be patient a little longer.

My breath turns to ice as I walk home through the rain . . a little cloud escaping my lips and becoming part of the night. Warm light comes from the front room as I round the block to Sandra's house. It's the second house from the corner . . same as all the others . . side by side all down the avenue . . identical houses sharing walls and ceilings and broken up only by intersections. Each hides the same secrets, I bet.

I see Alexi leaning against the door with a cigarette between her fingers. Her body is long like a branch. She's thin and sharp at every angle.

She pulls her hair into a bunch behind her neck when she sees me. She says hello by blinking her eyes. I catch the start of a smile that goes away before it ever shows.

"Is he here yet?" I ask.

"They dropped him off about an hour ago. He hasn't said a word since."

I lean to the side to peek in the window. "Has she said anything?"

"Other than bitch?" Alexi says, giving a tiny shake of her head. "Nothing."

I tell her I'm going to go in and she tells me to do whatever I want by smiling long enough for it to show this time.

I know where he is without anyone telling me. Sandra had us clear out our stuff from the room off the hallway last night and then had us throw a sleeping bag on the floor for him. I know he's in there before I even get to the door because that's the only place he'd feel safe . . the only place he'd feel shut away from the rest of us.

Everything inside me feels funny . . that first day of kindergarten feeling . . like my legs are falling asleep but wanting to run as fast as they can at the same time. I feel like I'm the new one in the house even though it doesn't make any sense to feel that way.

The door is open but I don't show myself yet. I stay just out of sight.

I think Alexi is annoyed at me . . that I care at all about meeting him.

Last night, she told me, "It's no big thing, Kid. They come and they go all the time." But I've never had one move in. I've always been the one to show up . . the new gift from the stork dressed like a social worker.

My voice jumps out of me when I see him flash by the space between the door and the wall. He hears me and his face appears in the doorway. It's nothing like the photograph lost in the shuffle of papers on the kitchen table. There's life in his eyes.

"Hey." His voice is a low whisper, like the cough of a dog.

I can still feel the rain on my lips when I smile . . the last drops trickling down the side of my face as I wipe them away with a tiny wave, hoping he thinks the redness in my cheeks is from the wind.

"Hi," I say . . pushing my tongue to the roof of my mouth . . bringing my eyes down to keep from watching him step back into the room. His hand catches on the door to drag it open. An invitation to follow him as he sits down on the floor.

Most of him is lost in his clothes. The shape of his legs is hidden in jeans that are too big. The outline of his ribcage is lost somewhere in the worn out gray of his shirt.

"I'm Dune," he says. I can tell he's careful not to look too long at me as he folds his legs under him. I think it's cute the way he starts to play with the corner of the sleeping bag. He feels the same need to do something with his hands as I do.

"I'm Elizabeth," I say. My voice gets stronger the closer I get to him. "But everybody just calls me Kid."

"Kid, huh?" He says it more to himself than to me . . getting his ears used to the sound.

"Yeah." I move over in front of the light so that he blinks when he looks up at me. "Looks like we should be friends." I point to the floor where it looks like my shadow is sitting in his lap. "My shadow seems to think you're okay anyway." I shrug my shoulders to make it sound unimportant even though my breath is coming and going as fast as my heart under my skin.

"That sounds alright by me," he says.

I don't mean to . . don't try to . . but it happens anyway. I smile wide enough to show him my front teeth that are bigger than the rest . . my bunny teeth . . that's what Alexi calls them. I always try to hide them even though she says they're *adorable*.

I wouldn't ever let him see if it wasn't there in his eyes . . the spark of a shooting star deep under the surface like a ship still burning on the bottom of the sea. I can tell he tries to hide it as much as I try to hide my smile . . but he's no good at it or maybe I'm just too good at seeing things in people.

Sandra shouts my name from the kitchen, making it sound like a curse word.

"Guess I better go," I say softly.

There's no need to look over my shoulder . . I can feel his eyes following me as I leave the room.

My eyes stay wide open as I lie in bed that night . . watching the headlights crawl across the ceiling as they pass on the street outside . . some faster and some slower . . streaks that dance like lightning in our room. I've never been able to sleep very well. Even as a baby my mom said I never slept. She said it was because it never gets dark enough for sleep in the city. It never gets quiet enough either. There's always the hum of the traffic, the noise of machines and the noise of the sidewalks.

It all spirals around me . . swirling like so much space around the sun . . leaving me in the center of it all . . like being spun up inside a spider's web . . only not as soft . . but the same sort of tightening feeling.

I can feel Alexi breathing . . the slow rise and fall of her belly against my arm. It's too fast for her to be asleep.

"Alexi." I whisper it so it can be lost if she wants it to be.

I'm ready to cover my mouth with my hands to keep from saying anything else when she makes a sound like the beginning of a word, letting me know it's okay to talk.

"What do you think happened . . you know . . to get him away from his home?" I'm asking the ceiling as much as her . . asking the stars that are invisible through the house and above the cover of light that hangs over the city. I trace an imaginary line to connect them . . trying to connect my thoughts . . trying to figure out how he was sent to me . . if he's a wish come true or just another runaway.

"Jesus, Kid." Alexi sighs, then lets out a breath and rolls over on her side to face away from me. "You're both like stray dogs . . just can't keep yourself from sniffing out each other. Go wake him up if you want to know so much about him."

I should've known it was a mistake.

I should've known I'd brought him up too many times already.

I slip the rest of me back beneath the sheets . . my knees like a perfect fit against the back of her knees . . my arms like a sleeve over hers until our wrists meet . . until our tattoo eyes touch and she can forgive me.

"Still love me?" I tease. She smiles before pushing me away. But gentle . . playing . . nothing mean about the way she does it.

"Yeah, right." She says it like she doesn't mean it . . but means it even more in the way she tries to hide it.

She's always telling me I'm the only one who's ever let her burn as bright as she wants. Back when she lived in Kentucky all they ever did was try to throw dirt over her to put out the flames.

She says she can't wait to be famous and have everybody see her the same way she looks reflected in my eyes. She always promises to take care of me once it comes true.

I place my hand on her neck . . let her hand rest on my head. Somehow the way our skin feels against each other helps us dream. It helps us forget.

I wonder if it's the same with Dune.

I wonder if he's like us . . if where he comes from is something he's trying to never remember. I wonder if his eyes are open now in the near dark . . if his face is turned up to the ceiling like mine to watch the dance of head-lights . . pushing away any memory of the past before it has a chance to grow.

"How long do you think he'll stay?" I ask.

"Until he gets caught," Alexi says. "Two weeks maybe."

She's probably right. He seems too soft somehow to ever be a good thief.

I say goodnight by letting my cheek brush up against her shoulder. Then I close my eyes and try to disappear until morning.

KNOW NO EDUCATION

"Kid, your boyfriend wants to know when you're going to school," Alexi teases the next morning when I come into the den.

I don't understand what she means.

The sleep is still in my eyes.

She's lying across the sofa, her toes rubbing together for warmth.

Dune is dressed the same as last night . . same jeans that hide the skeleton shape of his legs . . same shirt the color of a snowstorm coming toward the city . . same brown eyes that show through the longer strands of his brown hair.

"School?" My tongue moves around the word like I'm saying a word in a foreign language for the first time and wondering if the way I pronounce it is funny to everyone who's listening to me.

"Yeah, you know," he says, "that place with kids and desks everywhere. Pencils, books, and teacher's dirty looks."

Alexi laughs once, then brings her attention back to the cartoons that flash across the television screen with amazing colors you never see in real life.

I walk over and see him watching my knees as they move in and out of sight from the bottom of the long shirt I wear at night . . watching me as I sit on the floor between the two of them.

"They told me I'd have to switch from George Washington Carver," he says, gesturing with his hand to where Brooklyn sits a dozen subway stops away. "That's fine with me though. I hated that place."

I glance over at him. I can tell by how his expression is far away that he's not just talking about the school. He's talking about the group home too. The night the social worker was here, Sandra said something about how he got beat up there a few times, which was why the social worker was so set on getting Sandra to take him in.

"So where do you guys go?" he asks. "I saw a public school a few blocks away when they brought me here. Is that it? I didn't get a good look but it seemed okay. Right?" He's asking all his questions faster because we stay silent. Alexi keeps her eyes on the television and I keep my eyes on his. I can't believe nobody told him.

34

"Don't you know?" I ask, hugging my legs.

His head shakes side to side. "Know what?" he says.

"We're *home-schooled*," I tell him, saying the last part with my hands waving on either side of my head like quotation marks. "Where'd you think Sandra went? She's there at the school right now to sign you out."

"Oh. I thought she went to work or something."

Alexi and I both laugh. The idea of Sandra working is as likely as the idea that the city could get turned into a desert overnight. She's never worked at anything except stealing . . and she doesn't even work at that anymore. She has us to do the work instead. That's our school.

The pieces of paper in the social workers' folders say she works at a car service, pushing buttons and answering phones. But those are just papers . . fakes like the report cards and lesson plans that are supposed to be taught at our kitchen table. They're all easy to get . . her uncle or cousin or somebody else with the same accent as her can get them as easy as buying something at the deli . . a whole network of fake stores with fake workers getting fake jobs. She says it's how the old country will take over ours.

Nobody checks. There's no reason for anybody to check as long as the papers look real.

"So, um, when do we start?" Dune asks after the minutes have ticked away and the cartoon is over. "Do we have books or anything like that?"

35

Alexi takes a sip of the coffee sitting on the table in front of her head . . lifting her head up enough only to swallow . . making a face at him as she rolls her eyes.

I flash a look at her.

It's not his fault he doesn't know anything.

She doesn't care though. She told Sandra she wouldn't have anything to do with him. She said she'd trained enough pickpockets in this house and wouldn't even think about another this soon to getting out. "Besides," she said, "this one here's my best student. She can do it."

So it's me who says to him, "We can start now if you want."

I stand up quick and snatch a notebook from the side table. It's about the same size as a wallet and I make sure to show it to him before I reach behind me, slip the notebook under my shirt and into the waistband of my underwear, and put my hands back at my sides.

"I'll close my eyes," I tell him. "Try to take it without letting me know."

Alexi mumbles about me not wasting any time . . teasing about dogs sniffing each other in an alley and that she'll need a hose soon by the look on Dune's face.

He sits stiff as I get ready to close my eyes . . get ready to feel him try not to touch me. But he doesn't even move to get up. He doesn't understand any of what we've said.

He will though. He'll learn.

I explain it to him. What we do.

He either doesn't get it or just doesn't believe it.

I explain it again.

Alexi can't stand to listen again. She gives me a look . . the one that says she told me he wasn't all that smart. Then she leaves the room.

Although I don't think he really understands it yet, he says he'll try. He does try. He's just not any good at it.

I feel him every time. His hand is clumsy below my spine. He pulls away too quick.

"You're too heavy when you move," I tell him. "You have to be like air." I glide my arm in front of him like the wing of a seagull. I show him how softly it moves.

He takes a step closer to me. His hand covers his mouth because he's nervous about bringing his face close enough to kiss me while his hand sneaks around the side of my hip . . down along my back like an imaginary friend . . perfect, just like I've been teaching him all morning and all afternoon . . perfect up to the crucial part . . the part where I feel his fingers move like tiny claws to grip the wallet in my back pocket.

"Fuck!" he shouts when I flinch at his touch. It sends chills through my ribcage. "This is stupid. I can't do this!"

I put my hand on his elbow.

"Hey, don't worry about it." I tell him we've only just started. It's only the first day.

There's something about being close to him that makes the eyes on my wrist feel like fire. I feel each heartbeat sending blood through the veins that run beneath it.

I never care about anyone for too long, it seems. Not after I'm used to them. Only Dune feels different somehow. He doesn't feel new.

"What if you get caught?" he asks. "I mean, how does this whole thing work?"

"You don't get caught," I say. This is rule number one. "You get caught and you're on your own. Bye-bye foster home and hello juvey." I'm not smiling now because this is the most serious thing he's got to know. Sandra isn't going to bail him out if he's busted. She's never going to put herself in the middle of it and risk getting caught and sent back to Russia. There, she says, her life isn't worth the ashes that she lets fall on the kitchen table every night.

Dune shakes his head and curses under his breath.

"You can never tell either," I say, my voice going faster as I say it. "Thief's Honor" . . a rule as old as stealing itself.

"I don't believe this shit," he groans. I can't really understand why he's so upset. I mean it's better . . better than school . . better than them telling us all these things we'll never need to know . . better than begging on the streets too . . having all those people looking down on you just to throw change in a cup because they want you to go away.

"Look," I promise him, "no one's going to make you go out there until you're ready. Don't worry about it."

He tells me that maybe he doesn't ever want to be ready.

For a moment I see everything that he tries to hide . . a quick flash behind his eyes.

"How long have you been away . . from your home, I mean."

"I don't know. Six months, maybe."

I knew it couldn't have been long. He hasn't learned the secret of being on your own yet . . hasn't learned to wear beauty like an armor that covers you from head to toe . . protects you the way superheroes protect themselves with shields and capes and things. Nothing can get in to hurt you once you learn that. Nothing will worry you too much either. That's what I have to teach him. Then he'll be able to move through crowded subways like a ghost.

I start to teach him by brushing the hair away from his eyes with the back of my hand . . the same way Alexi taught me . . teaching him by placing my mouth so close to his cheek that he can feel me breathe . . so I can feel his tiny hairs that tickle my lips . . but not close enough for it to be a kiss. He has to figure it out before I do.

"This sucks," he whispers.

"It's not so bad," I say. "You'll see. It seems unfair, but it's better than most anywhere else."

"How's that?" He sniffs up a laugh as he says it . . a laugh that is closer to a cry than it is to being anything near happiness. "It sounds like a prison. She controls everything you do."

"Who? Sandra?" I laugh to myself as I say it. Dune wants to know what the hell is so funny because it sure seems that way to him. "She doesn't control anything," I assure him. "She lets us do whatever we want as long as we give her what we take . . and that's nothing. It only takes like two hours a day for that."

The rest of the time we are as free as being on the streets . . free to live in a daydream . . wandering through the city like characters passing through the pages of a book. We are able to climb up to the stars and down to the bottom of the ocean every hour, if we want.

40

Nobody telling you anything you have to do.

Nobody to say anything about you is wrong.

Nobody trying to change you into what they want you to be.

"All you have to do is be alive," I tell him. "The life of a thief is the most beautiful way to live."

"If you say so," he mumbles. He's not really convinced . . not yet anyway. It takes time to adjust.

"Well, at least you'll learn a skill." I slap my hand against his knee and try to change the mood back to playing. "Good thieves never want for anything as long as they live," I say. These are the same words Alexi said to me.

I stand up with my arms at my side.

"Try again," I tell him, "this time without caring about getting it right or wrong."

I'm ready to practice for hours, so later when Sandra asks me how he's doing, I can tell her at least that he's getting better.

PART OF THE SCENERY

I'm not sure he's ready . . the way he paces back and forth a few yards away.

I told Sandra that but she wants him out as soon as she can get him out.

Wants him caught just as quick.

It's only been four days . . not enough time.

A group of girls lingers around . . waiting for someone to seek them out. I stand there disguised as one of them . . listen as their voices are taken away with the wind . . my hair caught in it too.

I stand perfectly still . . my hands in my pockets . . nothing that will make anybody suspect me of anything . . or even of being with him. I fit in so naturally at the edge. We're in front of this store that sells what's outside more than what's on the shelves. It sells the look of all of us gathered out front . . sells the young and pretty kids of the streets and the chance for the rich to get close to us.

I wonder if Dune gets what I've been trying to tell him the last few days. I hope seeing me stand with all these girls makes it clear how good we've got it.

I whistle like a songbird in the wind while I wait, and get a dirty look from the girl standing next me. Her hair has dyed pink curls. She wears a pink outfit like a second skin to show how much she's worth.

I hate being here . . hate remembering how people I used to know when I lived on the street had to do the same thing . . how they thought it better to sell their beauty instead of begging for change.

I'd walk off any other time but it's the best place for Dune to practice because anyone we rob here won't dare report it to the cops if we get caught.

It's an easy set-up too. Letting him be a decoy.

It'll keep him from getting caught. It'll keep Sandra from sending him away.

I shouldn't care so much . . but he's so scared. He told me so yesterday. He was almost in tears talking about getting sent to juvenile hall. His hands shook even after he shoved them under his legs to hide them.

I promised him that his life wouldn't get screwed up just because of Sandra. And I promised myself that I won't let him down the way so many other people who've made promises to me have let me down.

A man in a dark suit walks closer. It's the walk of a target, and I know Dune sees it too. It's time.

Dune steps away from the wall . . right into the path of the man in the dark suit.

I only taught this strategy to him yesterday but it never fails. Alexi taught it to me way back . . made me the decoy the first few times out. I made the perfect one . . cute and young and easy to yell at. I only had to go into a store with dirty feet and dirty hair . . bump into customers and knock things down . . watch the guys behind the counter build up fire in their lungs until they yelled . . chasing me away with their words as Alexi grabbed whatever her fingers had time to touch.

It's like slow motion when their legs get tangled . . feet tripping each other and their hands go up. The man waves around to catch his balance and puts his hands out in front of him to stop his fall.

First test passed perfectly.

"What the fuck's the matter with you?" the man shouts, his mouth twisted in an angry snarl. The girls near me all stand up straight and fall around them.

"Fuck you! What's the matter with *you*?" Dune shouts. I can hear the nervousness in his voice like he's trying to remember his lines. But the guy won't know this. Especially when Dune remembers how it's supposed to work and shoves the guy just a little as he's getting up.

That's when everyone comes alive. The girls sing words of surprise with tongues licking their lipstick. Some shout at the man to leave Dune alone. And some shout at Dune to leave the man alone, because the man's a paying customer, and Dune's just a thing of the street like them.

My turn next.

My turn to slide between the others. To get up behind the guy.

One easy motion is all it takes. One swipe of the hand, light as air.

Jackpot.

His wallet is in my pocket before he even feels me grab his arm. I yell up at his face, "Leave him alone, asshole!" I make my voice high and crazy. I show my teeth like a dog ready to bite.

I bend down to help Dune. "C'mon, let's go," I say. I put my arm around his waist and use the other hand to pet his face like a girlfriend would. It's what my lines tell me to do.

The man doesn't say a thing. He doesn't have time as we start to walk down the street. We leave him to drown in the attention of girls who love his money . . money that's leaving with me.

The rise and fall of our lungs is like the stop and go of the crowd at a crosswalk in fast forward. Finally we slow down to normal speed as my heart stops pounding.

It's the first minute we've had to catch our breath since getting away . . since slipping around the corner with the speed of the traffic . . dipping into the subway station . . hopping the turnstile as the train pulled in . . *stand clear of the closing doors, please* . . and riding along the four stops before exiting and hopping on the next line to get downtown.

I lean back against the bench and push the hair away from my face. Drops of icy sweat keep it in place.

"Know something? That wasn't so bad," Dune says. His words are more of a surprise to him than me.

"I told you it wouldn't be." I tilt my head to the side. I

want to make him feel like he should believe everything I say when I smile and show my front teeth.

I take the wallet from my coat for the first time since we ran. My fingers flip through the bills . . hundreds . . four of them . . then four more twenties and a five and three ones.

"We're set," I say. "That was a good score. We don't have to do shit else the rest of today." I'm saying it up to the last leaves on the trees as much as to Dune.

"That guy was a dick anyway," Dune says. "It sort of felt good to take his money."

I remember when I first ran away . . how I used to beg for change with this girl Gretchen who sort of took care of me the way I'm taking care of Dune. I remember how she used to give the guys in suits dirty looks as they walked away after dropping a quarter or dollar or whatever in her hand. She told me how good it felt to take money away from them because they didn't care at all about us. They cared only enough to give what they didn't need.

Stealing is the same sort of thing, I guess.

The only difference is that the guys I take money from don't even care enough to give that much.

Gretchen never saw it like that. She'd get real mad if I ever stole anything. She said being a thief gave them reasons not to care.

I used to believe her too.

But I know now that she was wrong about that. Because they look at me like I'm total trash no matter what. So she was wrong to even care what they think at all . . because it doesn't matter how they see me . . doesn't matter what I show them on the outside . . as long as I keep shining inside they'll all see me someday . . see me the way I really am. Caring about what they think is like being kept in a cage.

I'd rather fly free.

I see it in Dune too . . still something small . . something that stays in the shade behind his eyes. But it's coming out . . waking up to being alive . . waking up from whatever crap he'd been told by all the people and things he ran from.

We'll start today.

Start right now.

I grab his hand and say "C'mon," pulling him up from the bench and into the wind so that his hair stands up straight. "The rest of the day is ours." I sing it out to the ocean . . to the sky . . to the people walking by who stop and give us looks because we are going to be everything they are not . . no rules . . no responsibilities . . the way we are all supposed to be.

I spread my arms like wings as I run through the park . . wondering if my feet will have to touch the ground forever or if I'll get picked up and carried off like a wish thrown into the river.

And when I look back over my shoulder I smile . . smile
not so much at the feeling but at the fact that Dune is feeling the same thing . . his hands gliding the same way.

I'm smiling because he never asks where we're going.

I'm smiling because he believes in me so completely.

The view from the ferry running between downtown and Staten Island is just as good as the one that actually goes to the Statue of Liberty. It doesn't stop at the statue but so what . . it doesn't cost fifteen dollars a person either and we just want to see the statue a little closer.

My stomach jumps with each wave . . the ship bouncing as it pushes the water aside like a clumsy swimmer.

I put my fingers up to my face to inhale the salt smell they catch in the air . . put them in my mouth to taste it. It's the same as tasting the rain or tasting dirt. It's so beautiful to have the world inside me.

Dune keeps his hands up to his face too . . but only to blow the cold away from them.

"You ever been there before?" he asks . . his head nodding in the direction of the statue standing out in front of us . . standing so tall in the water . . making little kids wonder how she doesn't sink because the waves rise and fall so high to hide the building she stands on.

I shake my head. "Never," I say.

"I went once," he says. "When I was little." It's like it's something he's not sure he wants to let escape from him but he lets it go anyway. "I went with my mom and dad and my little brother."

He quickly looks away. This is how he tells me he'd rather I didn't ask any questions.

He doesn't have to look away though. I wouldn't ask. It's part of being one of us. You never ask no matter how much you might want to know. You always wait for them to tell.

The birds circle above the boat, screaming out at us.

He clears his throat before he starts to talk again. "My dad." The way he says it tells me more than any story he could tell . . the way he says "dad" with a slight laugh . . saying it like his dad is a person who exists only in the past. "He told me and my brother that the Statue of Liberty was so tall because it had to be able to see all the way to the other side of the country. He said they used to tell immigrants that she was always watching them so they'd better not do anything wrong."

Nobody must have told that to Sandra when she got off.

"We used to believe everything he said," Dune tells me . . looking out over the water like the day he was here

54

in the past is somewhere just over the horizon . . that if he looks hard enough he'll be able see it . . be able to change how things happened. "He was so full of shit most of the time."

"My mom used to take me to the park we just left," I say. "She used to tell me the Statue of Liberty was really a goddess that came from heaven to watch wishes as they floated down the river and protect them as they made their way off to the end of the world."

I don't tell him about the rest of the story . . about telling my class the things she said . . about the way they laughed at me. He seems to know anyways. He takes one step to the side to stand that much closer to me.

"I guess all families are kind of fucked up, huh?" Dune folds his hands over the railing like he's waving to a fish we can't see.

"Not all," I say. I reach for his hand. It feels like ice against mine . . but safe at the same time. "Not ours." Not if we don't let it get that way.

I can tell it means something to him . . more than he shows. That's all any of us foster kids ever want . . a family that we belong to . . to be adopted by people who love us. But I know something he hasn't learned yet. I know that we are the ones who adopt each other. We are the only family we'll ever need.

"Let's go inside, out of the cold," I say, and he says it

sounds good to him. We've shivered enough out here . . shed enough of our past for today. It's time to leave it out on the deck . . let it get carried off into the ocean where it can't hurt anyone.

I turn around once before going inside where the benches are lined with tourists . . letting my eyes meet with hers as she holds the torch high over her head. I give her a quick wave just in case my mom was right . . in case maybe Dune's one of those wishes I made as a little kid. Because maybe it takes this long to get here. If it's true I don't want her taking him away for not believing.

It's the last good-bye before we fade into the crowd . . before we get back on the ferry going the other way . . a last daydream before heading into the night on a sub-way train headed to Queens.

PUPPY LOVE

"C'mon, Kid! Get up!"

I open my eyes and Alexi is stretched up tall above me. She's standing on the bed with her feet kicking me in the side until I wipe the sleep out of my eyes.

"Jesus, you're hard to wake!" she growls. Her skeleton arms shake me. The gray light from the window behind her is like a far away halo above her head.

"Stop kicking me!" I yell, grabbing her foot and pushing her away. "I'm up."

The storm outside is the only sound besides her laughing as I sit up. Just the rain hitting off the cars parked on the street . . tap-tapping as they break like soft glass on anything that's metal . . breaking beautifully.

"Get dressed," she says. Then she leans back against the dresser to watch . . telling me Sandra's gone out . . taken the day off. "She said something stupid about how even

59

terrorists need a day of rest and just left. We can do whatever the hell we want."

Everything about her is itching to be seen . . the way her arms are at her sides . . the way she smiles . . licking her pretty teeth clean.

Her eyes are like blinking neon lights as she watches me stand up . . electric around the edges.

"I invited Kinna over," she says, twisting a short strand of her hair around her finger . . winding it tight before twisting the other direction "I figured we could hang out and drink from Sandra's liquor cabinet." Her smile turns greedy. She loves days like this.

"Oh," I say, making a soft sound as I let the day play out in my head for a second. "Sounds fun." I smile to match the words coming from my mouth as I think about Kinna and Alexi . . about the way they like to watch me move around the room . . the way I sing for them while they make drink after drink in the kitchen.

Alexi starts early . . starts now by watching me slip off the clothes I sleep in . . the feel of her gaze traveling over my shoulder and down to my waist . . from my knees to my ankles and up again.

It feels dangerous to be so pretty trapped in her eyes.

She comes around behind me to put her hands down on my head . . running her fingers through my hair. She's careful not to hurt me as she pulls the knots out. Nobody ever wanted me forever the way Alexi does . . wanting to hold me near her wherever she goes. So I don't mind being like a doll for her sometimes. At least I know she'll never lose me that way.

The windows shake when the wind picks up.

I hear the howling as we step into the hallway . . bare feet on the floor like the rain falling against the roof . . and it all sounds the way the beating of my heart feels when I press my hand against my chest. Its same rhythm getting faster as the rain picks up . . faster when I see Dune sitting in the kitchen with his face in the shape of a question.

"Good morning," I say, putting my hands on my hips and making his thoughts stop dead in their tracks.

It's so easy to see through him that I almost feel bad.

Except that I don't . . because I like the way he gets nervous inside . . how seeing my shoulder blades naked causes him to clear his throat . . trying to make it look like he's not watching me . . not staring at me . . seeing the beginning of wings take shape beneath my skin.

"Jesus," Alexi says, stepping between us. "Somebody get the puppy a bone to keep him from drooling all over the place."

Dune closes his mouth and looks down at his hands instead of at me.

I try to hide my smiling. She's been teasing him all week . . ever since he got here . . teasing him about being my pet. I don't really like when she does it. It's not fair to him . . and I actually think she'd sort of like him if she gave him a chance. But the way he's sitting there . . just like a puppy begging to be taken for a walk or something . . makes it seem to fit, and I can't help letting out a small laugh.

"What's going on? What are you guys doing?" he asks once he's finally got the courage up to speak.

"Nothing with you," Alexi snaps . . glancing over at me and making her eyes narrow . . icy sharp . . reminding me what she said last night about how I've been spending too much time with him. She said I was getting too attached . . but what she really meant was that I wasn't spending enough time with her.

"We're just hanging out," I say, pushing myself up close to him. I say it nicer than it needs to be . . trying to make up for her.

He barely looks at me when she's in the room. He's afraid of being teased some more. He keeps his head down until I reach over and move the hair out of his face . . letting that say everything.

I know he thinks it's a competition between her and him.

I don't know how to tell him so that he'll understand. It's nothing like that. We're all the same. We're all family. I tried to tell him yesterday when he asked me what her problem was . . tried to explain how Alexi will warm up to him eventually . . that she's just a little jealous is all . . that she doesn't like anyone new in her life . . not at first.

He asked if she liked me at first.

I told him "Of course," but that being a girl makes all the difference with her.

We both follow the bend of her elbows as she takes three glasses from the sink. She rinses them under cold water before placing them in a straight line on the counter. One for me . . her . . and Kinna.

"Don't you have any friends or nothing?" she says, turning to Dune and shooing him from the room.

I let my hand brush up against his leg as I whisper for him to ignore her. I ask her to rinse out one more glass "for our brother" . . batting my eyelashes at her and getting her to laugh as she lifts another glass from the sink, saying he can rinse it out himself.

I leave the last sip in the bottom of the glass dangling over the sink . . letting the water run . . ready to fill it up clear once I swallow the last taste of whiskey . . the taste of dragon breath . . ready for a cold drink of water to put out the fire all down the inside of my chest.

"You still working on that first one, girl?" Kinna asks. Wrinkles show up in her forehead when she raises her eyebrows . . glitter eye shadow twinkling like pink lightning on her skin.

I nod my head as she lifts her glass up to her mouth and takes a sip as easily as taking a breath. Her eyes open so wide the white part glows against her dark skin. It's pretty like snow falling on mud.

"Longer you wait to finish that, harder it's gonna be," she says, her tone making it feel like there's forever between our ages . . between just being fifteen and nearly becoming eighteen.

Even the smell of it starts to make my stomach sink . . every inch of my body begging me to leave it right where it is.

"C'mon now." Kinna's begging the opposite of me . . saying it like she's talking to a little kid. I love the way she talks . . like the words come from somewhere so deep inside her that they come out too slow.

I toss my head back and let fire drain into my throat.

I come up coughing for air . . bring my hands up in front of me and try to catch my breath. All of a sudden everything inside begins to move so fast . . rushing around like traffic as the room rocks side to side so slightly that I can't be sure if it's really moving or if I'm imagining it. I'm not sure even after it begins to pass.

"Damn, that's what I'm saying." Kinna laughs . . slaps her hand down on the table when I lean against the counter with an empty glass . . wiping the corner of my mouth with the back of my hand before smiling. She says she thinks it's cute the way I get when we're all drinking.

I tell her I like it too.

I like the way it makes me soft inside like a cloud floating up to heaven.

For a moment none of us makes a noise and the music

takes over in the empty spaces . . the stereo in the other room . . the singer firing off words like a weapon . . ugly and angry like gunshots in a nearby building . . but then a woman's voice soars over his . . her song like a bird in the sky . . stronger than the meanness . . a beautiful sound that covers his like giant wings to protect the world from the heat of the sun.

Notes crawling over my skin like friendly bugs.

Her voice finding its way into the center of my bones.

The song all swollen inside me . . getting stronger like a cramp or a stomachache until it has to come out . . starting off small but getting bigger . . all the same words as the ones coming through the radio wires . . like the song is something that has to come out or it will kill me. I close my eyes and let my voice fill the room. It feels so strange . . like my soul is leaving and my body has no way to keep it in.

Time stops with the sound of my voice.

It's frozen until I grow quiet again . . silenced by the return of gunshots killing the pretty part of the song.

"Sorry," I whisper when I open my eyes. All of them are staring at me . . but as soon as I apologize they laugh, because I know they don't mind when I sing . . at least they tell me that . . tell me they love the sound of my voice. But still it makes me shy.

Even Dune is smiling a little bit. It makes me feel good

to see him like that because he hasn't fit in with whatever we've been doing all day. It makes me feel warm somehow to know that I could cause that . . a different sort of warm than the alcohol . . a better one.

"You're gonna make us all rich one day with that voice," Kinna says.

"Maybe," I say. But I don't know. Alexi's the one who'll be a star. I only like to sing for myself . . only when it builds up in me to where I can't swallow it back down. They wish I'd sing more.

Alexi slides up beside me with the bottle in her hand. "Ready for another?" she says and pours my glass full again without waiting for me to answer. Her other arm's around my waist, her hand far out away to keep from burning me with her cigarette.

"Cheers," she says. Her eyes are red like firecrackers in the rain. The alcohol smells sweet on her breath . . mixing with the smell of her lipstick . . vanilla and kiwi and I wish the whiskey tasted like her instead.

I take another sip . . the smallest sip that I can. It feels the way running from the cops feels. It feels the way hiding in my closet felt when I was young.

There's a feeling in my stomach like something bad is about to happen when I swallow . . racy and nervous the way my heart is beating. It passes as quickly as it comes though . . leaving just the warmth behind.

"It's so much work," I say.

"What's that?" Alexi brings her hand up to my face to catch a drop dripping from my chin.

"Getting drunk," I tell her . . making my face into a frown at the terrible taste on my tongue as Alexi, Kinna, and I all start to laugh.

From that moment on it seems like everything we say is funny. Each syllable is a joke worth telling. The way we move our mouths is hilarious. It feels so wonderful to be happy about nothing at all.

I look over at Dune sitting near the door . . slumped over with his elbows on his knees. I wish I could make him feel it too . . wish I could explain it to him, but whenever I try it doesn't come out right. The words get lost.

I take a step closer to him as Kinna and Alexi take a step away . . their arms around each other's waists . . lost in whatever their eyes are saying to each other as their teeth touch when their tongues glide over each other's as quickly as snakes.

"Dune . . come here." I hold my hand out to him like I'm asking him for a dance. I hold out the last sip from my glass like an invitation. He only gives me a little grin when he shakes his head, saying "nah," that he doesn't like to drink and hates to dance even more.

I see Alexi out of the corner of my eye . . Kinna's hand closed around her wrist . . her skin like a shadow . . Alexi's pale and paper thin. She's watching what he does . . the look in her eyes like having her fingers crossed . . hoping he doesn't get up . . that he doesn't come near me . . a mean smile when he stays seated.

"Hey, Dune," she shouts, snapping her fingers to get his attention. "If I throw a stick for you, will you go away?"

I feel her hand on my back . . fingers tracing the notches of my spine as she comes up beside me . . burning the skin on my wrist when the eyes of our tattoos know they are close together.

"She's only gonna break your heart," she says . . her cheek pressed up near mine as she says it . . my bottom lip tucked under my teeth trying to keep her from saying anything else . . anything that might come too close to the truth because I'm actually a little scared of the same thing . . of breaking his heart the way it seems I break everyone's heart who gets too close to me.

"Alexi . . stop," I say. But the words don't mean anything. Not when her hand slips further down my back.

When she kisses me behind the ear I have to hold my breath . . close my eyes to keep any sound from coming out. I pinch myself in the side and bite down harder to keep from letting it show on my face how good it feels inside because I know it will hurt him if I do. It would be telling him that Alexi wins and he loses.

He stands up when Alexi turns back to him with the

69

taste of my skin on her lips. She chases him out of the room without saying another word.

Or maybe he leaves because I don't say a word.

"You shouldn't have done that," I tell her when he's gone. She makes a face at me and says that he'll still follow me around at my feet if that's what I'm worried about.

"What . . you like that boy better than you like us?" Kinna asks.

I shake my head. I just think it's hard for him and I remember when it used to be hard for me.

"No? Then get over here, Kiddo." Kinna holds her arms out to hug me . . saying I've got too much sadness in my face . . that she'll make it go away. Part of me wants to follow Dune to where he's shut the door to close us out . . part of me wants to let Alexi and Kinna try their best to make me forget he was ever in the room.

I'm pulled in both directions as I spin around . . not knowing which is right and which is wrong until I'm finally too lost to care. I'm lost in the song that comes through the speakers. I'm lost in their arms that pull me toward the counter where their hands help lift me up.

He lies so still on the sleeping bag that I wonder if he's awake . . if his eyes are open in the dark . . watching me walk toward him or drifting off into somewhere else in a dream.

I close the door behind me . . making sure it clicks so it won't creak open again if Alexi or Kinna or Sandra (who's home now) walks by.

Light from the living room creeps in under the crack . . the blue glow of the television flashing the news on Sandra's sleeping face. It's the same news as every day so I don't know why she insists on watching it every night. I never saw the point of it. I only ever cared about the news when I first ran away . . watching through store windows for my face to show up . . fingers crossed so tight, hoping it wouldn't . . wool hat pulled down almost over my eyes so

71

nobody else standing around would recognize me if my picture did show up on the screen.

It never did . . not any time that I watched, anyway.

I knew some kids who watched were hoping for the other way . . hoping some smiling picture of them would light up the city . . tears in their parents' eyes begging for them to come home safe. It all depends on why you left, I guess.

When the light hits Dune's eyes they glow like cat eyes . . shining only for a second so that I can see they're open as he lifts himself up . . half sitting . . half sleeping.

"Kid?" He says my name in the startled voice of someone woken suddenly. "What're you doing?" His head looks around for clues as I kneel down next to him.

It's only been ten days since he came to live here but it feels like so much has changed since the first time I did this . . since the first time I came to his room with a smile on my face trying to get him to like me. It feels like our whole lives have been spent together in that time . . even though I know nothing about him . . only little things like the name of the town he's from in New Jersey before his parents moved to Brooklyn. I know how many people were in his family . . his father and mother and little brother . . know some stories about his friends and other stuff like that . . but nothing about why he's here or why he left.

He knows less about me. He knows nothing, really.

But those are things that don't matter . . not to me, any-ways. What matters are the things that you can't tell . . the things that just show on you like stains below the surface that show the color of what's inside you.

I can see those things in him. It's like seeing his soul instead of his skeleton. I can see the way his body is like a rainbow . . beautiful and striped from his face and his stomach and down to his knees and ankles. I can see it the same way he can see my butterfly wings.

I guess that's sort of why I snuck in here . . to make sure he can . . to make sure he sees what I want to show him. I want to let him see the inside of my heart instead of what he saw in the kitchen earlier.

Late at night when my mom used to come into my room this way, she'd tell me stories of things I didn't understand. She used to tell me that we all lived a different life before this one . . that we lived over and over . . that after we die we float around on a long journey back to being born into someone else but that all the people we meet are all the same people we knew before . . and that even if we can't remember, our souls never forget.

Everyone always told me she was crazy. But some of the things she used to whisper in the dark seem true to me.

I crawl onto the sleeping bag beside Dune. I only let one finger touch his hand as I say, "Hey."

"What're you doing?" I can feel his whole body get tight . . each muscle tense like a statue under his clothes as he pushes himself away. He pushes his body against the wall like I'm something dangerous. He covers the rainbow inside him with ashes.

"It's okay," I whisper. "I won't bite."

But I guess he's still sort of mad at me because he doesn't laugh or smile or even change his voice into something nicer. "Look, what do you want?" he says, keeping the space between our bodies empty.

"Nothing." I put my hands up to my mouth. I wonder if I'm wrong. Maybe he doesn't see anything in me. "I don't know. I guess I wanted to say sorry." I'm sorry I didn't stick up for him more in front of Kinna and Alexi. I'm sorry for not telling him earlier what days like this are always like.

I feel him forgive me when his arm relaxes. His hand touches mine so lightly that it could be mistaken for an accident.

"Does she know you're in here?"

"Who?"

"Alexi."

"She's passed out, snoring in bed."

Picturing that in his head makes him laugh to himself. It makes him laugh a little more when I say he wouldn't find it so funny if he had to sleep next to her.

We don't speak again for a while. We listen to the cars

74

on the street. We listen to the shouts of the neighbors on the other side of the wall at his back. We listen with our palms pressed together . . listen like we are ghosts in their lives . . somewhere on the other side of the wall but aware of everything they say.

No matter how loud their voices get . . how angry their words . . we still feel safe from it . . safe lying next to each other. I guess that's what I'd want to tell him if the words could find their way out . . if they weren't buried so deep inside of me. I'd want to tell him that he makes me feel safe . . makes me feel the way I felt hiding under the sheets in the laundry room of my parents' house . . safely wrapped in their sour scent . . knowing my dad wouldn't be able to hurt me because he'd never find me.

Dune asks me why I hang around her. He asks me why I let Alexi treat me that way. He says I let her treat me like I'm nothing.

"It's the total opposite," I say. "She treats me like I'm everything." I pull my knees up to my chest and hold them . . remembering the way her hand feels when she pets me behind the ear . . remembering the way her eyes light up whenever she sees me. "It's just that she gets kind of protective. She loves me."

Nobody who's ever loved me has stuck around so long.

Nobody who's ever loved me has wanted to hold on as tight as she does.

I hold my wrist up into the light coming in the window, showing him the mask that stains my skin. "See this?"

I wait for him to nod. He says he's noticed it before. I ask him if he knows what it means and he shakes his head.

"It means we'll always be family. Me and Alexi."

He casts his eyes down to stare at the space where my hair falls against his shoulder . . looking sad until I tell him he'll get one too . . as long as he promises not to leave.

"Then you'll understand," I promise. "Then you'll be family forever too."

He doesn't say anything. He doesn't need to. I can feel how fast the thoughts are turning over in his head . . feel them as they make his pulse quicken . . make his skin warm to the touch.

I brush the hair away from his face with my hand and pet him softly behind the ear, whispering good night as I pull myself up and leave in the shadows, the same way I came in.

THE GHOST OF TIMES SQUARE

Neon lights shine on the sidewalks and off the towering glass buildings just as brightly during the day in Times Square as they do at night. It's an electric playground that never stops blinking with the flash of cameras held by tourists staring up at the sky.

I'm sick of it. There's no room to walk between the people who cover every inch of sidewalk. I need to slide up between them like a snake . . slithering in and out . . pausing every few feet to grab a present . . grabbing another wallet from another tourist.

We make our way like this from 55th Street down to 43rd Street . . a day's work in a few city blocks. It's the dance of thieves . . a miracle of crowds that makes everything so easy.

Dune has trouble keeping up . . keeping from bumping

into people we pass. He's out of breath when I finally stop to grab his hand.

I pull back the zipper and let him take a look in my backpack. There are at least ten of them in there. Some are thin with nothing. Others are so full the green tips of dollar bills stick out the top. It's more than plenty. The dirty plant smell of cash fills the air.

I close the backpack up as fast as it takes for pictures to change on the giant television screen hanging in the sky in front of us. "How'd you do?" I ask, putting my fingers near my mouth in excitement when he reaches into his coat. His hand holds the first wallet he's ever taken.

I remember the first wallet I ever took. It was way before Sandra and all of this . . way back when I was still on the street. I remember the way it made my hand tremble as I took it.

Gretchen got pissed at me the whole rest of the day.

I remember feeling guilty then.

It's funny how things can change.

"Not too good, I guess," he says, shrugging his shoulders as he looks down at it, like it's not worth the trouble it took to get it.

I tell him how wrong he is by placing a frozen kiss on his frozen cheek.

"What was that for?" he asks. The wind hides how pink

his face gets . . hiding the little mark of my lipstick but never wiping it off.

"Because you didn't get caught. It makes you one of us now." I feel the itch of my tattoo wanting to spread to him . . wanting to mark him right here . . not wanting to wait for Sandra to do it later tonight. I have to settle for locking my arm with his . . for skipping over the crosswalk with the secret of what's going to happen later.

"Let's go in there," I say, pointing to the toy store on the other side of the street that promises the perfect place to hide. Inside are aisles that reach up to the ceiling . . shelves stacked with boxes of things that bring smiles to the faces of everybody that sees them . . amusement park rides that glitter and spin like the circus lights outside and keep all eyes off of us as we wander through like elves in Santa's toy shop.

The whole place smells like babies and plastic . . smells like kindergarten the way I remember making pictures out of paste and colored paper . . a contagious smell that makes me smile like I've just turned five years old again.

Dune doesn't smile. It's not because he doesn't want to. I can see he wants to . . a smile tucked away just under his expression . . looks so close you could touch it but never too sure if it'll actually swim up to the surface to take a peek at the world.

I like how he gets shy about feeling happy. It's the way most boys get. He's afraid he'd look too much like a girl or something if he shows the rainbow stripes hiding under his skin.

It's okay though. It shows enough through the touch of his hand when I press our palms together and lead him up the escalator.

I've learned to ignore all the looks of normal people . . the turned up faces they make whenever I'm in some place they don't think I belong in . . staring at the small rips in my jeans or the holes worn into my coat . . rolling their eyes at the way I give them stares back . . scrunching my nose up at them like telling them to go to hell.

We step off the moving stairs into a world taken over by dinosaurs and robots . . army figures and little boys screaming out pretend sounds of dying.

"I hate these toys," I say. "C'mon — let's go back there." I pull him on to where the colors change from green and blue to pink and white . . where the kids change from boys to girls and Dune's face turns a brighter shade of red. I'm trying to teach him not to give a shit about what anybody thinks.

"Are we here to take stuff?" Dune asks, and I hit him.

Not too hard, but hard enough to make him ask what I did it for.

"For being dumb," I tell him. I explain there's no way we're taking money from any of these people no matter how many mean looks they might give us. Stealing from them is only stealing from their kids. Taking their wallets only takes a toy out of a child's hands, and I don't steal from kids.

Dune says he's pretty sure some of the people we rip off on the street probably have kids too.

I tell him that's different. It's different if you can't see them. It's different when you only take money from people that look like they won't miss it.

"Whatever you say, Kid." He lets his hand run over the heads of stuffed animals as we walk. "I don't really get it. But you're the boss." He laughs.

"See? You *do* get it," I say. I fold my arms in front of me and put my foot down like I'm stomping out any doubt he might have . . showing him how in charge I am as I smile.

I can't really explain what I mean . . about how the toys I had were the only things that really made me happy when I was little . . how when I made up stories for them to act out it was the only time I could escape.

But when he picks up a stuffed cat it's like he knows

without saying . . because of all the ones in all of the bins he picks out the one I had.

"Her name was Kitty Catrina," I say, taking the cat from his hands. "I got her for my third birthday."

"Oh," he says, like an apology.

"It's okay," I say, giving her a hug before putting her back on the shelf. And for a minute I worry he thinks I'm crazy . . until he does the same sort of thing . . until he stops to look at a bear that wears a top hat. He sees it and it's like his batteries run down.

"My brother had one of these." He says it like it's something he tried to forget.

When he comes back from his memories he says he wants to go. He doesn't wait for me to respond before he heads off in the direction of the exit.

I take one step before pausing and look in both directions. I take a deep breath and put the bear in my bag. Then I take the cat to keep it company.

The train sends blue sparks shooting out as it rumbles through the tunnels . . winding its way through the ground like a worm. It keeps us safe inside its belly . . safe from the electricity that makes it run.

But it doesn't keep us safe from what we carry along.

It can't keep out what's already inside.

I watch the wet streaks stain his face as he begins to rain . . as he sniffs up his voice while he says it was his fault.

"I didn't mean to," I say. "I was just . ."

But he stops me with a shake of his head and a small voice that says it's okay even though it's making him upset to hold the bear in his hands.

He says it was his fault about his brother.

I tell him there's no way he could have known there was a car coming.

"I was watching him though. I should've . . I don't know . . should've done something," he says. He says he was older . . he knew the city was different from where they moved from . . that his brother wasn't used to it yet . . to all the traffic.

Everything he's tried to hide from me comes out in his voice.

I never would've taken it if I'd known . . if he'd told me any of this before . . about how his little brother got killed by a car screaming through a traffic light . . never slowing down . . never touching the brakes even once as Dune watched it disappear into the Brooklyn afternoon. The way he stares out the window of the subway, it's like he's still watching it . . wondering why it wasn't him instead.

"Might as well have been me though, as far as my parents were concerned. The way they ignored me after that, I guess it kind of was."

There's so much I want to say, but nothing comes out. Just a feeling like a lump in the back of my throat that stays there.

"It's okay," is all I can find to say when I really want to convince him it wasn't his fault . . that nothing like that could ever be anyone's fault besides the driver's.

I put my hand on his and gently take the bear away. I hold it in my lap to keep it from hurting him anymore.

He wipes his eyes and says sorry, says it's stupid, because it was two years ago and it shouldn't matter anymore.

I find the words to tell him that's not true. I tell him not to blame himself the same way Gretchen told me not to blame myself for what my dad did. "It's not your fault," I say. "It doesn't matter if your parents said that." Because I know . . because he always said it was my fault too . . that I deserved it when he hit me.

But it was always his fault. He was always wrong.

And Dune's parents are always going to be wrong for making him feel dead because of an accident . . for not wanting him anymore . . for making him a ghost just like his brother and for not even caring when he ran away . . for not caring when he was found . . for saying it was maybe better if he stayed in the group home and abandoning him there.

All these other people riding the train wouldn't understand that . . wouldn't believe he was telling the truth if he told them . . wouldn't want to believe that anyone would leave their kid like that.

I do though.

I know it can happen because I've been left before. I know how it feels to have the only people in the world who are supposed to care for you just up and leave.

It's the same thing that Gretchen did to me when she left . . told me she'd be right back . . promised with a little wave of her hand . . said she'd let me sleep, walked out the door, and never returned.

I put my hand on Dune's back . . move it up and down . . gently but hard enough for him to feel it through his coat. Because I know how it feels to be told you're not wanted anymore . . when the people you love don't love you anymore.

He told me his story because it was hurting him.

I need to tell him mine so he knows he's not alone.

I whisper it all to him . . tell him how I went out to look for Gretchen in the streets of Chinatown where we were staying . . about checking every place we usually went to and not finding any trace of her . . about how she promised to take me with her if she ever left the city.

"What happened?" he asks . . and I don't mind telling him because it seems to help . . seems to make him feel better, and I don't mind feeling a little worse to make that happen.

"I went back . . to the place we were staying and everything . ." I have to swallow it back for a second before going on. I haven't told anybody in so long and I didn't think it would still be this tough. "When I got there . . she was gone." I throw my arms out to the side like it's the end of the story.

I guess it might as well be. She was gone from my life

after that . . nothing of her left . . none of our things . . nothing except the memories I try to forget.

"The woman we rented the room from said Gretchen came back when I was out looking for her . . said she took all of our stuff and was gone," I say.

I don't tell him about the money because I never tell anyone.

It only makes them feel sorry for me if I tell that part.

I don't like anyone feeling that way for me so I just leave that part out . . about how she took all the money we'd saved . . how she left me with nothing . . how she turned me into a thief that way. Not because of the money, but because she stole away the promises she made.

I wipe the corners of my eyes, clear my throat, and finish the story to the end. "The lady said she didn't want me hanging around either . . that we were trouble or something. So now I'm here."

I can tell he's about to try to say something comforting . . but I stop him because as soon as we start feeling bad for each other we let all of them win.

"And so are you," I tell him, grabbing both of his hands and getting my face close to his . . making him stare at me . . making sure he gets what I'm trying to tell him . . that none of them matter because they're gone and we're not. "We have each other now," I say. "We're not going anywhere."

Soon it'll be in his blood . . the ink that makes us relatives forever.

"Thanks, Kid," he says, coughing it all away. He takes the stuffed bear back from me and puts it in his coat, saying how it's like an angel and that he's glad I took it for him. Maybe having it close will keep his little brother near him somehow.

I tell him it's pretty to think of it that way . . about keeping it close to his heart the way he is.

We stay silent for the next few stops, huddled together like if we stay close enough we'll be able to suffocate the past. We let it get off one memory at a time . . one station at a time . . leaving pieces of us scattered all over Queens.

SECOND TIME AROUND

"SO WHAT!" Alexi shouts, her hands balled up into fists at Sandra, who keeps asking over and over again how she could be so stupid.

"Look how bright it is!" Sandra screams, pointing at Alexi's pink dyed hair.

I curl the ends of my own hair around my finger as I watch Alexi parade back and forth in front of the kitchen table . . wanting to tear all the hair from her head and make a pretty pink rope to strangle Sandra with.

It's been going on for at least an hour, ever since Alexi got home with her hair shining like the neon lights in Times Square . . making the blonde streaks that are left look white . . bleached and bright . . beautiful the way the two colors mix like a peppermint after it's been slobbered on . . after the red fades to pink.

I put my fingers up to my mouth . . touching the tip of

my hair to my tongue. "I like it," I say. Alexi pauses to wink at me between explosions of fists and tugs at her head.

"Everyone will see you!" Sandra shouts, leaning so far back in her chair that I hold my breath for a second thinking it will tip until she leans forward again to tap ashes onto the table.

"I don't care!" Alexi cries. "I WANT everybody to see me!" She straightens her spine as she stands . . arching her back and turning her head to the side . . chin on her shoulder to stare at me . . giving us her star pose.

I smile at her to let her know she's as pretty as ever . . prettier even. My smile's a little shy when Sandra's watching . . but big enough to let Alexi know I'm on her side.

Sandra taps furiously on her cigarette . . tapping off the lit end as she mumbles to herself . . cursing and stuff . . saying how being famous is every little girl's dream but it's a wasted one . . saying there are a million girls just like her. "You want everyone to notice you," she spits out, "but the only people who are going to notice are the people you're stealing from."

"Whatever." Alexi rolls her eyes and turns her back on Sandra.

"This was that colored girl's idea, wasn't it?" Sandra says. "You have her change it back tomorrow!"

"Colored girl?" Alexi's face is scrunched up like she

can't decide whether she's more angry at what Sandra's said or glad she's been given a reason to attack again. "What year is this? Racist!"

I feel myself fading into the wallpaper . . drifting away as they come closer . . facing off like snakes waiting to bite . . Sandra the calm one . . laying back with a sway of her head to ignore her enemy . . Alexi like a snake with sharper teeth . . slithering and hissing. Each is careful of the other one's tricks.

"Don't call me if you get caught," Sandra says. There's a quick flick of a lighter to get smoke in her voice again.

Same threat as always.

Same answer too.

"Maybe I just won't steal again." Alexi shrugs her shoulders as she says it.

I bite down on my fingernails as I watch them. It's been the same argument every week I've lived here, but I love watching it. I love the way it makes my stomach flutter. I love the way it makes Alexi's eyes glow red . . even more now with the new color of her hair. Her arms get strong even though they are so skinny . . skinny enough to slip out of any handcuffs or between any bars if she ever did get caught.

One day she's going to win. Once she's eighteen there's nothing Sandra will be able to do. They both know it, which is why each time they fight I see Alexi get a little bit closer . . see her teeth a little clearer . . sharper . . waiting for the day when she actually bites.

Today it all gets broken up though when Dune walks into the room . . standing in the doorway and clearing his throat to interrupt the two of them facing off.

"Um . . there's a Mrs. Garrison at the door." He says her name like he's not sure if he got it right. "She says she's from Child Services."

Sandra drops her cigarette in the sink. "Well, let her in," she says to Dune, shaking her head at how helpless she thinks he is.

Turning back to Alexi she tells her she wants her hair back the way it was. "Tomorrow . . understand?"

The social worker shows up in the doorway just in time to see Alexi grab at the ends of her hair one last time . . to hear her scream "FUCK YOU!" at the top of her lungs before storming off.

Everything about Sandra changes. She sheds her old skin and slips into one that's more polite. She looks at the social worker, raises an eyebrow, and says, "Her hair is bright pink . . what am I to do?" The lady laughs, saying she understands because she has two teenagers of her own.

I give a little laugh . . and cover my mouth when they look at me.

"You're here to check on the boy, right?" Sandra asks.

96

"I'll get him in here." She calls out Dune's name with a soft way of saying it . . with a need to be nicer than she's been before.

The woman puts her hands up in the air for Sandra to stop. "Actually, I'm here for . . Elizabeth?" My name is like a question as she reads it off the paper in her hand. "That wasn't her was it? With the pink hair?"

My breath freezes inside me at Sandra's stare. "Not to worry," she says, pointing to me. "That's her there." When the social worker says she'd like to talk to me alone, Sandra says she'll step out to the store and give us some privacy.

I go cold all of a sudden at the thought of being left alone . . because answering the social worker's questions is like going to the doctor. I know there's nothing to worry about but I'm scared all the same.

The woman thanks Sandra and waits for her to shrink away before sliding out the chair from under the table, sitting across from me, and painting a smile on her face. She opens my file to check over a thing or two before saying, "Shall we begin?"

I take a deep breath . . ready to lie.

"Sure," I say. Then I smile politely . . the way she expects me to.

As soon as she starts talking, I know this isn't the regular routine. Her list of questions isn't the one I've answered every month for over a year.

It's something different this time. She makes that clear from the start. "I've got some news that you and I need to discuss" is how she puts it. The look on her face turns serious in an instant.

I want to cover my ears with the palms of my hands and shut out the sound of her voice. I try my best to ignore her when she tells me about my dad.

I nod and pretend to listen.

How long did she say? Thirty days?

Thirty days is all that's left . . thirty days until she says my dad is up for parole.

It makes my heart stop . . counting thirty days into the

future. All I can picture is him holding my hand against the radiator next to the expensive plate I dropped . . holding it there until the skin on my palms blistered and turned to black . . an ugly burned color . . nothing like the soft color of Kinna's cheeks.

It still feels so close to me even though it was a long time ago now.

"Elizabeth," she says, "I know this is hard." I keep nodding . . keep my hands tucked under my knees to hide them . . to keep them safe from anything that burns. "But we have to decide. The parole board's going to need to know if you want to testify. Either way, for or against. It's up to you. Do you understand?"

I keep nodding. Not because I understand, but because I can't bring myself to do anything else.

It feels like the trial all over again . . sitting here feels the same as sitting on the stand with my dad's lawyer calling me a liar. Not using that word, but saying it in other ways . . making up stories and things . . saying things about me that weren't true . . not 100% true anyway . . not exactly the way they happened.

He said I used to tell lies to my teachers all the time. He said I used to tell stories in class about drowning in the river and how the seagulls saved me . . stories about being dead before and being born over and over . . getting it all wrong because those were things my mom said to me . . things I was only repeating . . things they all took the wrong way.

My mom wasn't there to stand up for me. Just like always, she missed the whole thing. She was already in the hospital . . the "loony bin" is how my dad's lawyer put it with no objection from anyone. He asked the jury if it was possible that a crazy mother could have a crazy daughter.

He offered proof.

He read a list of things about me that he said showed all the signs. Me wetting the bed. My "imaginary friends" that weren't imaginary at all because they were real toys that you could touch and see. He told them how I ran away . . "a sign of an unstable personality." He said living on the streets for two years could put "wild stories in a child's head."

They weren't stories though.

They were all real things he did. He made all of those things happen and that's why they sent him away.

I don't want to tell those things again.

I told them once and thought that was enough to last forever. Now it's expiring in thirty more days.

"Elizabeth, you also need to know that he's made a request to become your legal guardian again."

It's like her words reach into me and steal all the air out of my lungs.

"But . . I thought . . I mean he can't . ." I can't think of how to say it . . about how they promised me I'd never have to see him again if I didn't want to . . how they told me he would never be my dad again.

She must know without me actually saying it, because she puts her hand on my shoulder right away. She makes a soft sound like *shhhh shhh* to a baby . . saying not to worry . . that it's totally up to me . . that she just needed to make me aware of his request.

"No," I say.

No to everything.

No to speaking for or against. No to ever facing him again. No to anything she has to say. "No" until she goes away and I can fold my arms and put my head down on the table and go back to being as happy as I was before she showed up.

She licks her finger before flipping through more papers . . more records of my life that the city thinks are important. Her chipped red nail polish flicks through things I'd rather forget before stopping on the one she wants me to remember.

"It's just that . . because you were so young," she starts . . trying to make it sound like she isn't just learning

101

these things. "Only eleven years old when you ran away" . . lowering her shoulders to bring her face to mine . . leaning forward to close the gap where I'm slouching away. "Eleven," she repeats with wider eyes this time.

Eleven years old doesn't sound so young to me.

Eleven years felt like a long time to wait before I walked out.

If she knew she wouldn't think so either . . if she had been there instead of just reading about it now.

It's like I wasn't even born until then . . until I became like everybody's little sister in the squats . . treating me the way family is supposed to . . letting me be me . . free and beautiful the way they said I was always meant to be.

"Maybe the way you saw things then aren't the same as you'd see them now," she says. "People can change, Elizabeth."

When I saw my dad again for the first time . . when I woke up in the hospital . . he said then that I'd changed. "My goddamned daughter's a beggar," he spat, and the way he said it made it sound worse than all the other things he always thought I was. Worse than being a clumsy brat. Worse than being a little bitch. Worse because it made him look bad to have me looking poor.

There's nothing he can do to me now. Not if I never see him again.

"No" is all I tell her . . all she has the right to know.

I don't understand why she gets like she's angry at me . . why she thinks she knows better than I do when she says how important it is for me to speak to the parole board. I wonder if it's for my good or for the good of all the paperwork she has in front of her.

"No," I say. "I don't want to." Because I don't care if he gets out as long I don't have to see the way he looks at me.

"Okay. Like I said, it's your choice." She's not even looking at me when she says it, making it clear that she thinks I'm making the wrong choice.

I wish Alexi were in here with me . . wish she was here because she would tell this woman to FUCK OFF. She would scream at her about how she doesn't know anything about anything.

It makes me braver just thinking about having Alexi near me . . makes me strong enough to cross my arms and lean back the way she would . . tuck my lower lip under my teeth and make my eyes small and angry to let this woman know she's welcome to leave now. I'm done talking.

"I suppose you don't want to know about your mom," she says when she sees the way I'm glaring at her. She's trying to prove I'm not as tough as I might think I am.

"No . . I mean, yeah, I want to know." I hate her the most for making me ask.

Her face lights up again with all the fake niceness she

came here with. She tells me the doctors say my mom's doing well. She says it's good for me to care . . but saying it so that it makes it sound like it's wrong that I don't care about the parole hearing or my dad or any of that other stuff.

"Will they ever let me see her?" I ask. My hands are shaking so hard that I have to tuck them tighter under my arms. My words are trembling too but there's no way to hide them except to swallow and bite down harder on my lip.

The social worker shakes her head sadly . . the soft look of her eyes that comes with bringing bad news . . so well trained like they have handbooks on how to deal with these things . . so forced and fake that I don't fall for it even for one second because living on the streets teaches you to see through those things.

"I'm sorry," she tells me. Alexi says it's all an act . . that they all feel bad for us when they first start doing this job but get tired of it after a while . . get to hate all of us after a while . . thinking we're all just fuck ups with attitude problems . . think of us as needy brats the same as most of our parents did.

"Fine," I say, and go back to glaring. I don't understand what the point was of bringing it up if it's the same thing as always.

It's not like I'm heartbroken . . like I'm going to run into the next room and start crying or anything like that. I'm not like some of those other kids I've known living on the streets . . the ones who would go back to everything they left for just one hug from their mommy.

I'm not even sure I want to see her . . but it would be nice to know I could in case I ever did.

"They say it wouldn't be good for her. Not right now," the woman says. "I'm sure they know what's best for her." I don't know how it could be "best for her" to keep thinking I'm dead . . to keep believing something she made up.

Before the woman leaves she tells me she wants me to think it over some more. She'll be back in three weeks for my final decision even though I've already given it to her so many times.

I only mumble when she says good-bye. I see the fake smile pop back on her face as she goes to the next room and begins talking to Sandra, who's back from the store with a fresh pack of cigarettes and diet soda. The social worker whispers to her all the things she's already told me.

Dune comes into the kitchen, dirty socks sliding on the dirty floor.

"Everything okay?" he asks.

The skin on his wrist is still red and scabbed from the stab marks of the heated pen. The scab hides the blue ink in his veins. It's a mask over the mask that will come off in a day or two and make him part of my true family.

"It will be," I say. Then I smile, showing him my bunny teeth, because it's already starting to feel better as I start forgetting about my dad all over again.

SHOPLIFTERS OF THE WORLD

My fingers flip through the CDs . . stop here and there. I pick one up to look at the cover . . to read the back before putting it down again. The feeling I usually have isn't there . . no stares crawling over my skin. Nobody is watching me.

They're all looking at Alexi as she stands like a skinny ballerina in front of the counter . . one leg bent while the other holds straight . . one hand behind her back while the other taps the counter to the music coming through the speakers.

And Sandra was all wrong about her hair. Not about everybody noticing it, but wrong about how it wouldn't be good for us. It pulls them to her like a magnet . . all the guys working in the record store . . each of them dreaming of being the one who gets to fall in love with her.

She lets all of them think it might be them.

I smile from the other end of the store at how stupid boys can be.

I keep a finger pressed to my mouth as I read the titles printed on the covers . . stopping at this one or that one with a title that sounds like something I might want to pretend to like. I take my finger from my mouth and touch the letters. I watch the florescent lights turn the traces of my saliva into rainbows on the plastic.

My other hand is the one doing the important part . . grabbing handfuls at a time and dropping them in my open backpack.

"What's this you're playing?" Alexi asks, pointing her finger into the air where the sound swims all through the store.

My hands move faster . . filling up the space in my bag like feeding a hungry animal . . stuffing its mouth to fill up its belly until it can't eat anymore.

There's a sudden sound of a thousand raindrops falling at once and everything stops.

The shattering plastic catches all of our attention . . making my hands stop . . making the guys behind the counter snap their necks around . . making Alexi's eyes glow red when they come to Dune a few rows over from me with a stack of CD cases on the floor in front of his feet.

I shake my head and look away . . looking as annoyed as

the rest of them . . careful to keep the secret that we are all together.

"Sorry," I hear him say to the guys as he bends over to pick up the fallen CDs and place them all back where they go.

To be a great thief you have to take advantage of every accident . . and I'm the best of all three of us, so that's exactly what I do. I take the moment to grab the collector's editions that are put up on display . . the expensive stuff . . feeding it to my bag with a hidden excitement . . a warm burn in the center of my stomach . . an itch between the veins in my wrist.

Alexi settles the place by making her eyes shine like stars.

It's the right thing to do when he walks out . . chased out like a dog caught begging . . head down and tail tucked between his legs . . face still red from being clumsy . . from the annoyed looks passed by the guys who just barely let themselves look away from Alexi.

I don't wait much longer after him. My bag's already full, anyways. I sweep around the aisles one last time, picking out a last one before wrinkling my nose at it to let anyone watching know that nothing here interests me.

I walk past them with my hands folded . . my lips pink and pretty and slightly parted as I sing softly . . not the song they're listening to . . a simpler one . . a child's

111

song so that the only thought they have about me is how cute I am.

Outside Dune is already pacing farther up the block . . not able to keep any part of him still as his hands keep fumbling in and out of his pockets . . bringing them up to his face to blow on before shoving them back. He kicks stones on the sidewalk. His hair is blown back by the wind as he keeps cursing himself under his breath.

"I screwed up, didn't I?" he asks when I get close enough.

I pull him to sit on the steps of the nearest building and I shake my head. "Actually, you made it easier for me," I say. But I guess I don't sound too convincing because he stands back up again to start pacing, same as before.

"She's going to KILL me." He tilts his head all the way back to shout at the sun . . hoping it can shine bright enough to erase the mistake he made.

"She won't even care." I wave my hand at him like what he's saying is the craziest thing I've ever heard. But I know I'm lying . . I know Alexi's going to come out of there steaming from her ears once she's done playing her part.

Checking through my bag there's more than I thought at first . . must be thirty or forty of them . . at least $100 worth when we sell them . . maybe $200 if any of those expensive ones are really worth something.

That's the thing with shoplifting . . you never know what you're going to get. It's a lot easier pickpocketing, but doing that all the time gets boring. Besides, with three of us shoplifting's easier to get away with.

"Did you get anything?" I ask him. "I mean, before?"

"Before I fucked up? Yeah."

His hands swing the backpack off his shoulder. When he opens it, the sun reflects off the foil lining, blinding me with the rays that bounce back. The foil is what makes it so easy for us to get away. The alarm signals bouncing back same as the sun does.

His bag isn't as full as mine, but it's much better than I would've thought. Another $50, maybe.

It doesn't seem like it's going to matter with Alexi though.

"Fucking retard!" she screams as she comes toward us. She smacks him on the back of the head as she gets up behind him. "You fucked up the whole thing, you fuck-ing idiot."

"Sorry . . they slipped," he says. The sun on his face bleaches out all the colors beneath his skin, making him look colder. "I guess I was nervous."

She's not listening to him though. She doesn't want to hear it because she just wants to be able to tell me later how she was right about how we never should have brought him along.

113

"It wasn't that bad," I say, showing her that we got enough anyway.

"Oh, big surprise. Kid takes the side of her pet boy-friend!" She throws her arms up and throws her stare at me. "I'll alert the news — they can put it in huge print. KID STICKS UP FOR THE RETARD AGAIN." She's snarling at me like she's never done before.

She knows right away that she's hurt me. When she looks at me again I think she's going to apologize but she only takes a deep breath. No "sorry" in her voice but at least she stops shouting . . her way of telling me to forget about it as she takes a look in the backpacks . . saying "not bad" but adding "could be better" so Dune knows he's still not off the hook as far as she's concerned.

She takes up my bag and slings it over her shoulder.

"Let's go get rid of this stuff," she says.

I'm still so surprised at the force of her anger that it's kind of hard to get going again.

Gregg's careful not to look at me . . careful to not fall for me trying to look sad . . careful not to get caught by the poor homeless kid spell I cast so easily on men like him.

Asshole.

He doesn't want to let himself feel bad for me . . doesn't want it getting in the way of business . . of him trying to cheat me same as I'm trying to cheat him.

"A hundred fifty," he says. "That's it." He places his hands flat on the counter and goes back to looking down at the newspaper he was reading when I came in.

"C'mon, Gregg, give me two hundred." I pout and fold my hands together like I'm praying. *"Please."*

Gregg's the kind of guy who is impossible to picture anywhere else but in the dingy little store he runs . . the kind of person who becomes part of the scenery. Even when he sleeps I bet he's slouched over that counter just like he always is when I come in here.

"Get off my back, Kid. Two hundred for this? I can't even sell half of this crap."

I come in here about once a month to sell him CDs I steal from someplace else. I think he's getting sick of seeing me.

I can see Dune and Alexi standing outside . . their reflections like shadows on the front window as the sun dips below the tops of the buildings.

$150 is never going to do.

I make my voice go especially sweet. "One seventy-five?" Like everything in the world depends on him not being so selfish.

Gregg folds up his newspaper with a snap of old words in the air. He narrows his eyes at me when he says he knows the CDs are stolen . . that he can't keep doing this.

"Never stopped you before," I say. I put my hands on my hips and make my voice small. Then the frown and the big sad eyes. Make him feel like an ugly wolf. Make him feel like he's hurting me.

"Kid, I got to look out for my store," he says. He tells me he can't keep buying lifted merchandise from a strung-out kid.

"That's shit!" I say.

Again he offers me $150 like he's doing me a favor. I reach at the stack of CDs and start putting them back in my bag . . telling him I'm going to go and sell them someplace else. He can make up whatever he wants about looking out for his store but it's all a lie . . he wants them as much as I want the money.

"Kid, wait," he says, holding up his hand. "One seventy-five, okay?"

"Yeah, fine." I smile at him again because I knew he was full of shit. But this time I don't smile like some dumb little girl trying to make him feel sorry for me. This time it's my real smile . . the one that lets him know I win.

I grab the money from him the same way a child grabs candy out of a stranger's hand. He starts in about how I shouldn't come around for awhile.

"Sure, whatever," I say over my shoulder as I walk out the door and into the twilight.

A cold wind blows against my face like a brand-new day. I have a Christmas morning look in my eyes, promising presents for each of us once we split up the money. We can start shopping for the things we want that are too hard for us to take.

Unfortunately it takes more than this to change Alexi's mood once she's got something inside of her. Even in the early evening sun her eyes still shine with electricity stolen from the clouds.

I try to take her hand but she yanks it away. She takes the money with a quick flick of her wrist as she turns her back on me.

I know what she wants me to do. She'd forgive me if I crawled up next to her and bent my head to let her touch me behind the ear . . if I leaned into her hand and let my lips touch her palm to tell her I love her. If I choose her over him, she'd be fine and everything would be fun like it's supposed to be.

I'm not going to though. I'm not going to pick sides between them.

I just want her to understand that I like having him as much as I like having her, the same way she likes having Kinna as much as she likes having me.

"Where are we going to?" Dune asks.

Alexi answers by making a face . . not wanting to be bothered to explain . . figuring she didn't want him along anyways so it's up to me to tell him what happens next.

"Wherever we want," I say. "We've got like sixty bucks each to spend."

"Don't we have to give this to Sandra?" he asks.

Alexi laughs . . turning her head around just long enough to call him a dumbass before stepping faster toward the dying day in front of us.

I explain about shopping days . . how Sandra gives us a few days here and there to get whatever things we think we need . . things the checks from the city are supposed to buy us . . new clothes and stuff like that.

He's still just as confused. "Couldn't we just keep some of the money we take everyday? I mean, save it up or something?"

"NO!" I shout . . stopping and pointing at him so that he has to stop too. "That's a rule. No saving."

Dune puts his hand on my shoulder and asks what I'm all upset about.

"Nothing . . it's stupid," I tell him. I speak softer, like saying I'm sorry for yelling. "Saving only causes problems. That's all."

I want to leave it at that. I want to forget about the whole day before this moment right now so we can start all over the way it was supposed to be. But Alexi isn't ready for that . . not yet . . and even Dune doesn't seem like he is either. It seems like he wants to know more.

"She didn't tell you, did she?" Alexi says. A smile passes across her mouth. She's found a bit of proof that she's more important.

My heart beats faster as she slides up next to him, hooks her elbow on his arm, and leans close like they're old friends.

"You see, little brother, once upon a time Kid here had this friend," she starts. Then she tells him about Gretchen

119

stealing the money we saved and how I promised never to save another penny again.

"It's nothing," I say, making my eyes say *please* because I want her to stop.

It's too late though . . or she's too pissed. Either way she goes on about it . . asks Dune if I told him about the other money . . the money put aside for me . . and he doesn't have to breathe a word because she can read it all over his face that I didn't.

"She didn't mention that either, huh? She didn't tell you that there's a little trust fund set up for her by the court?" She spreads her arms wide to make it seem like a fortune, which is more than it really is because really it's next to nothing. Enough, they said, to pay for college.

"Shut up." I say it too quiet though . . saying it from too far away as they stand so close together . . saying it like I know it won't help as she goes on . . telling him all of the plans we've ever made . . how she's going to adopt me once she's eighteen . . how me and her and Kinna are going to take off for California.

She's loving how each new thing she says seems to break Dune's heart. Each new secret draws him further away from me.

"And we're going to leave your ass back in Brooklyn or wherever you came from," she says. There's no longer anything friendly in her voice. She's no longer holding his arm but giving him a little shove instead. I know there's nothing I can say to make him feel better when he touches the tattoo on his wrist . . touching it like it's a broken promise. But it's nothing like that. I never meant to keep it from him. It's just that it never came up.

"Why are you doing this?" I ask her. I can feel my butterfly wings getting small . . feel them disappearing into my spine as I stand there watching her smile.

"I'm only telling him the truth. Isn't that what you wanted . . to make him part of everything?" she asks.

Dune keeps his head down as he walks away.

I was never going to leave him and now I don't know if he'll ever believe me when I tell him.

Everything about Alexi changes once she's got her way . . once she's sure I belong more to her and less to Dune. She comes up to me with her hand out . . with her hand coming up to pet me behind the ear . . telling me she's sorry in the only way she knows . . sure that I'll forgive her.

THERE WAS A TIME

My mom always told me I was too close to heaven . . never far enough away from where we are in between birth and death . . that I was like a dream that she knew would end too soon . . that would make her wake up before she was ready to give me up.

I'd listen to her cry by the side of my bed. She'd be curled up in a ball on the floor as she held her knees to her chest in the dark. She'd whisper stories about how it was all her fault . . touching each new bruise on my arm with her lips . . saying they would all go away once the angels weren't angry with her anymore . . once they forgave her for wanting to keep me.

"They didn't want me to have you. None of them wanted me to have you," she'd cry over and over again . . saying I was a mistake . . that the angels said I wasn't ready to be born . . quickly whispering the words until they would blend together . . until their sound got lost in the snot from her crying and I'd turn away . . roll over on my side and try to fall asleep so that I didn't have to listen anymore.

My back to her only made her cry louder . . sobbing in the dark with only the light from the hallway that crept under the crack below the door . . covering her mouth to hold the sound to a noise so low my dad wouldn't hear her.

"They wanted me to kill you . . to drown you inside me. They wanted me to give you back and I didn't. It's all my fault." She would fold her hands and pray out the window . . pray to the light in the windows across the street from our house.

Her hands were sweaty when she'd run them through my hair . . too quickly . . tugging the knots out but I didn't ever dare to make a sound. I didn't ever want her to know I was awake because that only made her cry longer . . louder . . only made my dad come down the hallway with fists full of anger.

When she thought I was sleeping she'd tell me not to be afraid . . that when the goddesses sent for me it would be the most beautiful thing . . that there wouldn't be any pain when the sky split in half . . parted down the middle to open a bright hole in the center.

Split like the sea is split in old stories.

"It will all be so pretty when they ride down on shooting stars," she'd say. I'd open my eyes as she spoke about them . . about the angels who she said were like little girls with giant butterfly wings colored brighter than the brightest sun in the brightest galaxy . . skin stained blue from the sky and eyes as green as leaves in summer.

Even in the dark, something about her face would shine when she spoke about it . . about the clouds thundering apart like a war storm . . about the sky swirling open . . spiraling faster and faster with the colors of a million butterfly wings wanting to swallow me . . about the little angel girls that would flutter through the storm . . their eyes twinkling like stars . . their hands reaching out for me.

"And you'll be the prettiest one of all," she'd say as I'd tuck my head under my arm and breathe the warm sour smell of my pajamas . . hide my thumb in my mouth to feel safe as she told me about how I'd put my arms over my head and twirl for them . . my toes in the dirt . . around and around until the air turned my skin to snow and my bones to ice . . until wings grew from my spine and opened up like the blossoms on the trees lining the street outside my window.

"That's when the stars will fall at your feet . . a thousand of them at a time like fireflies to wrap around you and carry you off." Her hand would stop moving through my hair when she got to the end. Her body would stay perfectly still and I'd see her start to open her eyes again.

Even when they would look on me, her eyes were always far away like she wasn't in the same world as me. If I spoke to her she'd grow pale like hearing the voice of a ghost. If I'd touch her she'd shrink away . . startled at first . . then fall all over me with her arms clutching at mine . . screaming to the imaginary visitors that lived in our house with us . . staying behind the walls . . showing themselves only to her.

She would scream for them not to take me away. "Leave me my baby . . leave her please." Over and over and holding me tighter with each word until it was hard for me to breathe . . until she began crushing my bones . . until my dad would come and drag her away . . yelling at me for whatever I'd done to upset her.

I'd lie in the dark and watch her crawl out of my bedroom . . wishing to myself that I'd never left . . that I'd stayed in heaven for her. Then I'd close my eyes and dream of the sky splitting open . . dream of a sky full of my mother's angels . . each of them perfect . . each of them coming down to see me . . their clean faces and shoulder blades like tiny birds . . too breakable to touch.

I used to wish they'd take me like my mom said they would.

That's what I wished for every time I blew an eyelash into the wind . . every time I crossed my fingers and shoved

them under my pillow before falling asleep . . wishing
they'd take me through the hole in the sky so she wouldn't
have to cry the next night.

Running away was like letting them carry me off.

Running away was like being born because the way we
lived was like being dead.

I don't know if it was that day or some day afterward
that they say she lost her mind all the way . . lost what
wasn't gone already . . sent the rest of her tumbling down
like buildings crumbling into dust at the end of the world.

It doesn't matter when it was though . . just that it happened . . that she believes in it . . believes they came for
me . . believes that I'm dead.

If I woke Alexi up right now and told her that I was
thinking about it again . . about all those times in my
bedroom . . she'd touch my face and tell me it was okay.
She'd tell me my mom was crazy to think all those
things. She'd tell me it's not my fault she was that way.

She'd put her hand on my chest to make me feel
alive . . move her fingers in slow motion circles to make
my heart race . . to feel it beating through her skin . .
pounding so hard until I felt the blood rushing through
my ears like a scream, shouting that I'm not dead . . that
I'm more alive than I ever was.

The feel of her tongue licking my cheek as her legs
would slide over mine would drown out all the other

sounds inside me . . all the doubt . . all the memories . . suffocating them with her body pressed against mine like a cure for everything.

But what if she doesn't want to make me better anymore?

What if she stops caring enough to be my medicine?

What if nobody ever cares for me long enough to keep me safe . . to keep me from becoming like my mom . . to keep from tumbling down . . breaking apart like dust on the street?

The light from a passing car streaks across my hand as I reach for her . . placing it on her shoulder until she stirs . . mumbles as she wakes.

She tells me to go back to sleep but I have to know . . have to hear her promise not to leave . . have to hear her say "forever" . . that she's never going to hate me like she did earlier today . . because I don't know that I can take it . . don't know that I'd last through her being mean to me.

"Alexi . . do you still like me?" I ask . . my words fading in the night . . getting weaker as they travel from me to her.

I know I shouldn't care . . that I should be mad at her for the way she told Dune those things . . but I can't help it. I'm too worried about losing her to be angry.

I cross my fingers because I'm afraid of the answer . . because everybody that I've ever been close to has ended up hating me . . because today was just like the last day I spent with Gretchen . . her drifting away from me, and me doing nothing to hold on.

"Huh?" It sounds more like a snore than a word as she rolls farther away . . the sound of her not wanting to answer . . not now . . maybe in the morning.

"Nothing . . nevermind," I whisper . . closing my eyes . . waiting for the sky to split open in a hundred cracks like the city is split by the avenues . . knowing that when I fall asleep I'll be that much closer to heaven.

MISTAKES ARE HARD TO MAKE

Dune's started tagging everything . . drawing a mask on park benches and the side of buildings . . in the subway and over advertisements posted on the sidewalk . . decorating everything the way our wrists are . . four quick strokes of a marker to leave a part of us behind everywhere.

The scrawl of a thief. A little souvenir to show where we've been.

That's what he says about the mark he makes.

If Sandra knew she'd probably freak. She'd turn him in or something . . get him sent back to the group home at the very least. She'd say something about how the tattoo is supposed to be kept a secret . . an old tradition where she comes from. Letting it out is bad luck. Leaving it on park benches is probably something altogether worse.

The marker comes out of his pocket like he's a murderer reaching for a gun. Then a quick wave of the wrist like he's pulling the trigger. The ink stain on the boardwalk is like blood from a bullet wound.

I don't bother saying anything to him about it today. I'm not sure he'd listen to me anyways. He hasn't really cared much for anything I've had to say for the past few days. Not since he started thinking I'm a liar.

"Aren't you even going to say something?" I ask his back as he stays bent over. His hand makes four quick strokes before he looks up at me . . only for a second . . only long enough to say "something" before looking away again.

"Fine," I huff. "If you don't want to talk about it, then I don't care." I'm tired of trying to bring it up. I can only tell him I'm sorry enough times before it makes me sick like wanting to throw up.

"Yeah, I don't want to talk about it," he says and goes right back to ignoring me.

I cross my arms and let out my breath loud so he knows he's not the only one who has the right to get pissed. He's just being stubborn is all . . not wanting to hear any of my reasons why I don't hate her.

Earlier on the train he asked me, "How can you even talk to her?" He was angry that I was sitting with her watching TV again . . that everything between me and her is okay . . which makes things not okay with me and him. He's spent almost three days giving me the silent treatment for the things Alexi told him . . and now he says he doesn't care about those things. Now he only hates me for not hating her.

I thought the whole thing was over when he said he believed that I was always going to tell him eventually.

I hoped we could all come out here to Coney Island and start over.

He only wants to start over if we start without her this time.

I'm tired of being in the middle though.

I'm not going to do it anymore.

I look out at the ocean rolling off the end of the world with the seagulls cawing and circling above . . their white feathers showing against the bluish gray of the sky . . their song getting lost in the winter waves.

I open my mouth to let the sound of what's inside me out . . the sound of the world stretched out so far in front of me . . rumble of the roller coaster lost behind me . . sound of footsteps of other lonely people walking the boardwalk in winter same as me.

When I start to sing they all disappear. The world dissolves like the colors on a painting left out in the rain. The apartment towers near the boardwalk melt away, taking with them all the ugliness they hide inside. I'm making my beauty strong again.

My song ends when I start to cough from the cold air tickling my throat. It ends when Dune puts his hand on mine . . the touch telling me to forget all that's happened to spoil all that's good between us the last few days.

He's got apology eyes when he looks at me. He tells me that I'm like a little bird when I sing. And I'm like a little girl, the way it made my cheeks turn red when I realized he was listening.

"Thanks," I whisper.

"I like when you sing," he says. "It made me feel stupid for acting like I was before."

I smile at him.

"C'mon," he says, pulling me toward the smell of popcorn and funnel cake . . toward funhouse mirrors and bumper cars.

It's easy for us to make it new again . . to erase the harsh looks and replace them with laughter. We ignore everyone else on the pier and let ourselves be free. We let our hearts be our tongues when we speak.

We spend our day like the ocean . . letting ourselves believe it's never ending . . that a new tide will never come in to change the way we feel right then . . happy believing it even if we know deep down that it never really works that way.

It's only after all the rides . . after the food and everything . . after the lights switch on as the sun begins to set . . it's only after all of that I try to tell him what I've been meaning to all day . . what I've tried to explain to him all week.

I tell him even though Alexi can be mean sometimes it doesn't change all the wonderful parts about her. It doesn't change the fact that she's the only person who's wanted me for forever.

In response I get silence and slow steps from him. I start to think the day has been undone again.

It's only him gathering his words though. Only a rest, not an ending.

"It's just that I worry about you," he says . . a shy way in his speech when he tells me . . getting out how he's worried about the way Alexi treats me . . saying there's something about it that bothers him . . that she just likes me as long as I make her feel good.

I tell him I know how it seems, but there's a lot he doesn't see.

The way her hands smelled like baby powder the first time she touched my face. The way her voice tastes like vanilla whenever I lick my lips and think of the things she whispers to me in the dark of our room. The way she makes me feel wanted by the promises she makes under the covers where she says everything is sacred.

Maybe he'll never understand. But that's okay as long as he trusts me too.

He's got sad eyes when I look over at him. I can't help but think that part of what Alexi says is true . . about him being like a puppy with me . . always wanting to protect me but not knowing enough yet to know how to do it.

I want to tell him to stop . . that he doesn't have to . . that I'm not his little sister or his little brother and he can stop worrying so much about what happens to me. I want to tell him that all the worry inside him will keep him from ever feeling happy. Worry like that is the kind I had with Gretchen. That kind of worry drove her away from me.

I don't dare say it though. It would break his heart if I said those things. He would think I was saying I don't need him when what I really mean is that I need him in a different way.

I'll let him be my watch dog a little longer . . keeping at my heels . . letting him bark when he thinks there's danger. If that's what will convince him that I'm not letting him go . . that I'm not running off to California . . that I meant all the things I said about family . . then it's okay with me.

When the time is right he'll understand that it's not so much one of us protecting the other. It's more about having a partner to watch out for you.

"We should get going," I say. The amusement park lights are glowing like electric candy that comes in too many flavors to count. We don't have the time to be hyp-

140

notized by them. We can't stay and watch the Ferris wheel spin through the salty air to leave its reflection way out on the breakers.

We are thieves with work to do. We set off into the Brooklyn streets with the heart of a wolf beating inside us. We have nothing to lose except each other, and the whole world to gain with a quick swipe of our fingers.

"Shit." I'm counting the money again as we walk . . but no matter how many times I count it there's not any more than last time. There's not nearly enough.

It'd be the third day in a row we've come up short if we go back now . . the fifth day this week. I think that's more than Sandra will let us get away with.

I forgot the wallets are never as full out in Brooklyn as they are in the city. Tens instead of twenties. Ones instead of fives. It makes all the difference.

"We have to get more," I say. There's no way around it. We're out of excuses that Sandra will listen to.

I look in both directions . . no one on the block except us.

We could still go into the city . . hop on the train and be in the middle of a crowd in half an hour if we want. We'd be late getting home . . but being late is better than

142

being short . . especially the way Sandra's been on his case. I think she's been harder on him since she noticed me and Alexi arguing . . mumbling more often about how boys are nothing but trouble . . her threats sounding a little more real than any I can remember.

Two people cross the intersection a little ways in front of us . . a man and a woman. The way they walk is like a dollar sign. It's like there's enough in their pockets to save us a trip all the way into the windy streets of Manhattan.

"The subway's this way," Dune says when I start walking toward them.

My head nods in the direction of the couple that is getting farther away.

"Them," I say.

I see the hesitation on his face . . asking me if I'm sure it's a good idea . . just two of them and two of us and no group to get lost in once we've grabbed what we need to take from them. He's pointing out to me all that I taught him to look for.

"You worry too much," I say. "Besides, I've got it all figured out." I drag him off in the direction of the traffic light, explaining as fast as I can what needs to be done to pull it off right . . how I'll get their attention . . tell them we're lost and ask if they know how to get back to the train.

"All you have to do is stand there and wait," I say, moving us along quicker . . around the corner with them in our sights again . . nobody else on the empty street . . just the way we need it to be. "Once they tell us, I'll give the guy a hug. When you see me pull away, it's because I got his wallet. That's when you grab her purse and run," I point out the empty lot we just passed and make sure he knows to head for there. Then we'll cut through back to the train.

"I don't know." He's shaking his head . . slowing our steps to hold me back. He wants to know why we're going to risk taking her purse if we get the wallet.

I show him the collection of small bills in my hand. "This is why. And unless you want to go all the way into the city, this is the easiest way to keep you from getting sent away." I can tell he's still not sure . . even after I tell him how easy it is . . how they'll get so startled that we'll be half way home before they even react.

"What if the train isn't there, Kid? What if they catch us?"

"They won't . . don't worry. And we'll just keep going if there's no train . . there's another station three blocks from there. Now come on." I grab for his hand and start to jog . . giving him a smile to make him brave . . not letting him say anything else to talk me out of it because I'm already shouting ahead, "Excuse me! Hey! Excuse me!"

When they turn around there's no other choice but to go ahead.

I give Dune a glance . . biting my lip and making sure he understands that everything will be fine as long as we stick to the plan.

I can tell he wants to argue about it some more . . but that he won't. This is part of him trusting me again. It's part of us being a team again no matter what.

They stop like cars braking for dogs running across the highway . . their eyes wide the same way . . watching us run at them and wondering if we bite. Checking out the way we look . . our clothes and everything . . and I can tell they're not as dumb as they seem . . that they know a little about what's up just by the looks they give each other . . looks they think I don't catch.

I have to pour it on to convince them. Sugar-sweet eyes. Lips pouted innocent like a baby. Even the way I walk needs to be planned. One leg in leg in front of the other with a little panic in my step. Quick breaths getting up close to them. Saying, "Thanks . . thank you . . we're *soooo* lost."

The nervousness disappears from their faces . . erased when they let their shoulders drop . . let themselves into my trap. *The wolf disguised as Little Red Riding Hood* is what Sandra says about me.

"We were just coming back from our friend's house . . she said to go this way but I think we went too far . . and we're just trying to get back to the city . . I have no idea where we are . . we're so lost." I spit it all out as fast as I can to keep them from asking specific things like where my friend lives or where in the city we're going.

My eyes follow the man's eyes as he gives us directions . . follow his hand gestures that tell me to turn right or left and wave off in directions I don't plan on going . . my head tilted back to look up at him . . making big eyes at him like a helpless stray . . nodding with each word he says.

"Got it?" he asks.

"Got it," I tell him with a wide smile coming over me. My arms spread like wings on a little bird as I wrap them around him . . so careful to make sure they slip under his coat from the very beginning . . not after, when it would be a dead giveaway.

I press my cheek into his chest . . the smell of pine like all men smell . . the smell of boys when they get too old . . the smell of my dad which makes it easier for me not to feel bad for letting my fingers slip in his pocket . . so easy and so professional.

"Thanks again." My words leaving a stain of saliva on his coat from the corner of my mouth as I pull away . . wallet in my left hand . . left hand in my coat pocket before either of us has time to take a breath.

I don't know if it's my fault or Dune's . . not sure which of us gives it away when we look at each other.

It only takes the smallest thing . . a wrong look in the eye . . an extra blink . . a tiny mistake that lets them know we're about to run. The woman holds on tighter to her purse and pulls away just the right amount . . just enough to make the strap break the wrong way.

The streetlights catch the falling things to make them sparkle like falling stars . . like shattered glass on the concrete . . a parade of coins and makeup and the flashing screen of her cell phone . . falling at the same speed that Dune falls . . tripped by cracks in the sidewalk . . nothing but his hands to hold him up.

The shouts are violent like the scrapes on his palms . . the skidding marks of his jeans as the cement skins his knees.

I'm stuck between him and the empty lot. I don't know whether to go or come back. I don't know whether he'll stand up or get caught.

It's all decided for me when the guy springs at Dune. Dune yells for me to run but my feet won't answer.

I cover my mouth same as the woman when the man's fist comes against bone . . like the crack of a car window struck by a baseball bat.

"STOP!" I pull my hands away from my mouth to give the sound a place to escape . . like ripping off a bandage to let my screams bleed . . shouting "LEAVE HIM ALONE" when a another fist bends Dune over . . twisting him at all the wrong angles.

I run a few steps toward them . . hold the wallet behind my head and throw it as far as I can . . yelling for him to take it back . . that he didn't have to get like that . . calling him an asshole for what he did . . for the way he looks at us like we're just greedy trash.

He has no idea.

None of them do.

None of them know what it means to live like we do . . to think every night you might get sent away . . or if not you then your only friends. None of them understand that a group home isn't any kind of home that they know . . that those places are like cages where the strongest animals tear apart the weaker ones.

It's only fucking money to them . . but it's freedom to us.

Dune crawls a few steps toward me when the man turns around to pick up his wallet. Then he picks up the cell phone and tells the woman to call the cops. He warns us to stay right where we are.

I help Dune on his feet . . help him off in the direction of the empty lot with the guy still yelling at us to stay put.

There's no time to ask him if he's okay . . no need to ask once we start running . . not full speed . . but fast enough as the woman tries to pick up the shimmering objects spilled over the concrete . . fast enough to be at the subway station long before any sirens race down the street.

Every part of me is shaking . . scared in a way I haven't been since I was too small to know any better. I'm scared that the cuts on his hands and face will be the things that take him away from me . . scared because I've never been caught and the feeling of almost getting caught might be worse.

And it's my turn to say "I'm sorry" . . to tell him he was right . . it was a stupid idea to try. Asking myself over and over how I could be so dumb.

He doesn't say for me to forget about it. He doesn't say it's okay or anything like that. He doesn't say anything. He only holds his side as we run for the green stairs that will take us underground. He keeps his fingers crossed for a train to come.

I look back real fast before we go down the stairs . . make sure they aren't following us.

The safe color of darkness blankets the street where we came from.

My feet dance down the steps . . so fast I don't feel them touch . . don't hear them over the rumble of the train pulling into the station . . the electric squeak of the breaks as we hop over the turnstile . . mechanical voice telling me to *stand clear* as I keep my body in the closing doors to give Dune time to get in the train.

I watch him as he sits down. He's bent over, folding himself away from me. I can feel my eyes getting weak as the stations go by.

Nothing got fixed today.

I only made things worse . . worse for him . . worse with Sandra too once we turn up like this.

I want to do what I've always done when I feel trapped . . to bite and kick my way out . . to tuck myself away by the river and ride it into the past.

"I'll tell her it was my fault," I say. "I'll take all the blame." I put my arm around him so he can rest his head on my shoulder. I tell him it's the only way. I hope it's enough.

And maybe it's because I'm not sure if this is the last time we'll be alone together . . or maybe it's because I just want to feel something other than all the things that are broken. I don't know why exactly . . but I know that whatever it is, I'm glad I don't stop him when he puts his hand against my cheek . . when he closes his eyes and kisses me for the first time.

Blue sparks of electricity inside me.

Blue sparks on the tracks as the train takes us away from the past.

Already feeling braver for his sake . . searching the subway car for new targets when I open my eyes.

"Don't worry," I say. "I'll take care of this."

CATCH A TIGER BY THE TOE

I sneak into his room before I leave.

He doesn't turn around right away when I come in and whisper *"hey"* softly like a bird.

Part of me wants to press my cheek against his shoulder blades until he turns around and he kisses me again like he did yesterday on the train.

But it would ruin everything if he did.

If Sandra knew, he'd be gone for sure.

Keeping us secret is the best way to stay together.

"She'll kill us if she knows you're in here," he says. His back is still turned and the tips of his ears are sticking out through the longer strands of his hair. He fumbles through a pile of clothes on the chair for a shirt to cover him . . something to hide the shape of the bones that make perfect lines in his skin . . beautiful and delicate like the metal beams that frame the glass towers in the center of the city.

"She's gone," I tell him. I hug the door frame, ready to leave if he tells me to . . wanting to stay and watch him get dressed.

Sandra's afraid we're spending too much time together. She thinks it's making me sloppy. And she knows I'm covering for him and keeping him from screwing up. One slip and he's gone.

One mistake and I might never see him again.

If she knew about the couple last night . . how they saw our faces and heard our voices and probably caught our names . . she'd have kicked him out for sure. What she does know is bad enough. $62 for a whole day from the both of us. That got her temper up . . circling around us like a snake . . slithering between the chairs . . each breath like the tail of a dragon as the smoke coiled around her face . . nasty stink in her voice telling him that wasn't good enough to earn the tattoo she gave him . . saying she could burn it off just as easy . . saying it to both of us.

It doesn't bother me much. I know in the end it evens out. One good day will cancel out the bad ones.

I'm worried about Dune though.

I don't know that he's ready to be alone out there. I'm not sure he can be a ghost in a crowd the way I can.

I'm afraid of him giving up. I want him to turn around and look at me as he gets dressed . . to see I'm worth trying for.

Taking off my armor to let him see what I protect inside when I tell him, "Even if we're apart all day, I promise to think about you."

Rainbow stripes show on his skin when my words pet his ear.

I reach into my backpack and take out the stuffed kitten I stole from the toy store. I put it on the little table next to where his sleeping bag is on the floor . . placing her just on the outside of his bag as I grab up the stuffed bear and put it in mine.

"There," I say. "I have part of you and you have part of me. That way she can't keep us separate."

As he takes hold of my waist . . not wanting to let go . .

I can feel how nervous he is.

"I better go," I say. I put my hand up and press my palm against his. My hand is so small in comparison. "Be careful," I add as I open the door. "Okay?"

And he says "okay" as I step into the hallway . . keeping my hand to my face as I walk through the living room . . covering my smile . . the television thundering against the walls of the empty room.

Keeping my fingers near my face even as I walk into the cold.

Keeping his smell alive as I walk into the sun.

Half a block away from the front door I feel her grab me from behind . . her hand like the mouth of an angry snake . . biting me with fingernails.

I nearly let myself scream but swallow the air when I see it's Alexi.

Fear turning into a surprise smile when I see her eyes glowing for me. "Got you," she says. Then she announces it's a Kidnap Kid Day . . a name she made up a long time ago for days everything gets blown off.

"I don't know," I mumble into my hand. The smell of soap from his hand is fading as the smell of smoke from hers takes over. It's the same scent of Sandra's threats . . same as the exhaust of the truck parked at the light next to where we stand . . dangerous to breathe too much in . . always spoiling everything in the end.

"What do you mean, you don't know?"Alexi says . . her

voice getting loud on certain words to make it clear she's only half joking. The other half is going to be pissed if I don't go with her.

"No backing out," she says. She tells me how she and Kinna have planned it all week . . a little party . . sort of a welcome back now that I don't have to spend every day with *him*. "We're going to have a real good time," she says, ending with a wink. She closes the space between us . . her knees to mine to make us Siamese.

The subway train rolls along the tracks above our heads . . pulling into the station ready to drag me into the city . . but too quick . . too many steps left to the stairs as it nears full stop . . following it with my eyes as the sky moves across the windows like pictures on a movie screen.

"I shouldn't." I make my voice as small as I can so the words get trampled under the tires of the cars that pass through the traffic light. I know I won't ever make the train if she doesn't let me go.

"Well, then I guess it's lucky you don't get to decide," she says. She pulls her hands from the pockets of her coat and reaches for mine. "That's why it's called kidnapping." She smiles as she wraps her fingers around mine . . the touch of ice in her fingertips as the train rumbles on its way without me.

I can feel each beat of my heart . . each breath of hers touching my mouth when she leans into me. Her body thin like a piece of paper that is so easy to tear . . but still so much stronger than me when our skin is like snow when we're wrapped up in each other.

"If I screw up again . ." I say. She runs her fingernails deeper into my skin to stop me from talking. I let myself go helpless as she places her fingers near my mouth to keep me from making excuses . . tracing the shape of my lips as I fold my hands behind my back and she opens her mouth.

"C'mon, Kid. It'll be fun, I promise," she says.

There's a small itch above my arm when she lifts my wrist . . brings it close enough to blow her breath on my skin . . saying I'm being selfish if I don't go with her . . that everything will work out just fine if I come along.

Today it won't though.

Her touching me won't relax me today. Touching me will make me think about him.

"I promised him." I speak to the ground and try to cover my words as soon as they get out. I try to keep my eyes from glancing back at the corner where our house sits just out of sight . . where he sits on his sleeping bag with a stuffed cat as his only friend in the world today.

"Who?" she barks . . wide eyes turning red around the corners . . following mine . . pushing off from me the slightest bit as she turns around . . quick fire in her when she looks back at me. "That fucking stray living in our house? Fuck him."

She lets go of me with a shove and disappears in the sun as she turns to the side . . wearing a shadow like clothing . . fading from view to take a deep breath . . to huff and puff and calm herself down before turning back again.

"Do you like him or something?" she asks. It's not the first time she's put it to me like that . . but it's the first time that there's nothing playful in the way she asks. For the first time she's afraid I might give her the answer she's afraid of.

"It's just . . he's got no one else," I sputter, hoping she gets how he depends on me the way I depend on her.

"Fine. Whatever."

I know she thinks it's stupid . . the way I see us. She told me to grow up the other night when I told her about how maybe all three of us could live together . . how we could be like a family. She told me she didn't want to be my mother or sister or anything like that . . and there certainly wasn't anyplace for him in what she wanted either.

I don't want her going away mad.

I want to try to explain it a different way. But I know that no matter which words I pick, she won't like what they mean.

"I'll probably have more fun with Kinna if you're not

159

there," she says. She's trying to make me jealous as she walks away . . trying to hurt me the way she thinks I'm trying to hurt her. She points at the next approaching subway train as she walks. "You better hurry . . you wouldn't want to miss it," she tells me. Every move she makes . . the way she swings her arms . . tilts her head to the side . . all of it's planned to make me guilty.

FOLLOWING DIRECTIONS

There's always someone around . . always brushing past you on their way to somewhere else . . scattering like a bunch of roaches at the flick of a light switch once the sun rises in the morning.

I've always seen the city that way.

Stepping out of the subway is like that.

Stepping into a crowd is like stepping into a movie without a part to play. I'm the only roach that doesn't know where the rest of them scatter off to.

I've never been a part of their world. I'm always a visitor . . an observer . . a little kid watching all the people passing by the front window.

My mother told me it was because I was born an angel . . too much of heaven left inside me to ever be like them.

Ideas like those are why my dad blamed me for having "no more sense than a savage" . . using his fists like medicine to cure me . . beat me until every word she filled me with would run out . . spilling over from me in tears and snot when I cried . . in blood when he wouldn't be as careful where he hurt me . . never saying he was sorry because it was his belief that savages needed training.

I think maybe I'm a little of both things. Angel and savage. A warrior with butterfly wings. Only here for a short time to wander the streets . . traveling through until the blue children fall from the sky to come for me. And when I go away the world will begin to end. Everything will come crashing down and everything new will rise up in its place. A different world in the blink of an eye once they build heaven around me.

That's what I like to believe.

Alexi says I'm just as crazy as my mom when I tell her those things. And maybe it *is* crazy. But I guess it's better to be crazy than believe all the shitty things that happen are all that there is . . that things never get any better than what I see around me.

I'd rather be dead forever than find out that is really true.

I spread my arms out as I walk . . smiling at the dirty looks from the people who step out of the way . . bending the world as easily as bending my arms . . twirling through them to catch the breeze on my face . . smile even as they curse at me because they'll never understand anything . . because they will always hate me . . but they'll never damage my wings.

I'll never be one of them.

I'll never let them cast a net wide enough to catch me. I'll do whatever I've got to and always get away. I'll beg, borrow, and steal forever. I'll let them have all things their way as long as they let me move through the crowds like a ghost.

Besides, I'm not the only one. We find each other in all the hidden corners of the city. All of the children who were born too close to heaven use our wings like shields. We stick together to keep them from making us as ugly as they are.

They try to break us apart. They use everything they've got . . the police . . Child Services . . laws and money . . all of it to trap us . . to get us to be like them . . to keep the songs out of our heads and to keep us from singing.

They drive us out into the open. They leave us with nothing left until we just give up and give our beauty to them for cheap.

They use us to destroy us.

Not me though. I won't let it happen to me.

I know all their tricks. They won't catch me again like they did when Gretchen left. And I won't let anything break us up like I did with her. I know better now and I will make Alexi understand. All of us need to stick together.

More than two is stronger than two. Wolves need to run in a pack.

She needs a little gift from me . . something to show her I don't love her any less just because I love Dune too. I'll pick a present for her . . wrap it up in my jacket and let her open it . . give it as proof that nothing will change between us.

I pass a table with items laid out for sale . . umbrellas and sunglasses and jewelry no one ever wears . . sold in a different language by the lady standing there. I slip beside her and wait for a question to be asked so she'll be distracted.

I pick the pair I want to get for Alexi . . sunglasses with lenses the color of the last fall leaves. I wrap my fingers around them as the lady looks in the other direction and I put them on like they've always been mine and walk away.

Nobody sees me. I move across the street into the maze of buildings stretching all around me . . making my way as the street numbers count down faster than the taxis drive in the packed streets . . cutting through the sea of black coats and high heels, ducking into office buildings . . lifting a wallet with a shy smile as I twirl too fast and bump into someone now and then.

I always smile . . always bite my lip. Let them dream about me all day. Let them pretend they can get close to me as I make my getaway.

Sandra has told us that when she was growing up the old people told all the kids that the spirits live in the wind . . blowing under your skin until your bones turn to powder. Those who weren't afraid of the wind were already with spirits inside them.

"Like you," she said to me. "The wind is good for a wolf. The wind is your friend. It's the cries of all the wolves that came before calling back to guide a safe route."

I go silent as I look out at the harbor.

The wind is telling me to stay right here.

As I hide my hands from the cold in my pockets, I can feel the sunglasses I stole for Alexi and the heavy fold of paper that makes other people feel like they're rich . . fills their heads with pictures like catalogs . . night-before-Christmas dreams of far away trips to far away places . . penthouses in the sky and all the things to fill them with.

But I don't want to buy any of those things. Money only buys me more time to be free.

Today I got more than enough to make up for any bad days I've had over the past week. I worked extra hard just to be sure. I never let one possible theft pass.

I hope Dune had a good day too. I have enough to cover him if he didn't.

My chest rises and falls with the waves. The pigeons and seagulls sitting on the wall are ready to carry my wish back once it's made.

I take a pen from my bag and pull one of the bills from my pocket. It's more valuable than the others. Does that mean it'll be more likely to grant me what I write?

My hand shakes as I hold the pen. It doesn't matter how clear they're written though. The river makes the ink like water anyway. The words don't have to get there in one piece. I learned that when I was five. All the letters can spill away because the wish written there is there for keeps.

I fold it over in careful triangles, then close it in my palm and say the words in my head.

I wish never to be left alone.

I toss it away to set it free.

I don't notice the little boy watching me until I'm done. The sleeves of his coat covering his hands down at his sides. I smile at him but he doesn't smile back at me . . not at first. Not until I bend my knees so I'm only as tall as him . . so that he can see my eyes are safe . . that the only thing I'm hiding is a pair of butterfly wings.

"How come you threw your money into the water?" His voice is small like the size of his mouth.

"Because," I say. I look around at the park for a hand held out for him . . for someone there to teach him things about making wishes and what's hiding in the noise the wind creates.

No one is though, so I guess it's up to me.

"You want to see?" I ask him. He nods his head up and down.

The way he walks is so delicate . . like each step would break his bones if he steps the wrong way. I wonder if I looked like this the first time Gretchen saw me.

His hand comes out of the sleeve . . the smell of paste and candy when his fingers touch mine . . sticky with the stuff all kids get into . . use it like glue to keep everyone from running away.

He climbs on my knee like something so easy to lift . . so hard to protect.

I realize then what Dune meant about his little brother . . about how even if it wasn't his fault it will always feel that way.

"Have you ever wanted something really really bad?" I ask him. He nods and I give the pen to him and ask if he knows how to write. I tell him not to worry when he frowns.

"Just scribble down whatever looks right," I say as I give him a dollar to make his wish on.

He won't do it though until I take one out for me too.

I show what I mean as I write another one . . watch as the pen makes loops and lines from his hand.

I stop him when he starts to tell me what he wished for. "It won't come true if you tell anyone," I warn him, the way my mother used to always remind me whenever I'd forget and start to tell her mine.

"Okay," he whispers, folding the paper like I folded mine.

I lift him up and let him toss it the best he can. He shakes with a quick happy scream as the paper floats away.

"Will my wish really come true?" he asks. I hear the same doubt that I always kept in my voice. He's giving me the same look I gave my mom when she promised it would.

I give him back the same promise she gave me.

"Mine already came true," I tell him with a smile. Then I smile at the woman coming up with a worried look on her face. She grabs his hand and picks him up.

She doesn't mean it when she thanks me . . telling the boy to come away even as she says it . . but that's okay because he sees the way I really am . . sees it when he waves.

I hear him tell her how wishes are made . . how I let him throw money into the river. She looks back at me and reminds him the rule about taking things from strangers.

"Nice to meet you!" I call out.

Hopping on the nearest train outside of the park, I hope my other wish happens just as fast.

I keep Dune's stuffed bear in my jacket the whole way . . hugging it close to my heart on the subway platform . . in the train . . keeping him close as I head into Queens.

I know that it was all worth it when I make my way around the corner and see Dune on the porch. I rush the rest of the way once he sees me . . letting out all the worry I saved up all day.

"You made it," I say when he's inches from me.

He locks his fingers with mine to let me know it wasn't as hard as he thought it would be.

"It's stupid," he says, his wrist touching mine. "But it was like you said. It was like you were there almost."

I tell him it's not stupid at all . . telling him by pressing my mouth to his quickly before going inside.

THINGS FALL APART

The sound of two cars colliding in the distance shatters the silence in the room . . metal twisting together with the crashing of windows. Somehow it's like the noise of glass breaking apart from the accident is the sound of everything Alexi wants to say to me when we look at each other. We're smashed up together so bad that I wonder if it can be fixed again.

I'm lying on our bed . . watching her walk in front of the window . . blocking the little bit of sun coming through as she drops her towel on the floor . . thin enough to be almost invisible . . just enough of her left to make a long shadow crawl across my hand resting so still on the sheet where she sleeps.

The sun paints her softly with orange light but I can still see the sharp edges in her skeleton . . the shape of her hips . . the staircase of her spine as she bends down.

I always want to give her part of me when I see her like that. I want for her to take whatever she needs so she won't look like her beauty is making her sick.

She always tells me I don't have any to spare . . putting her hands on my chest and moving them down along my sides to show I'm only small myself. But still I'm nothing like her. Her bones are hollow like the bones of birds.

I don't bother saying anything to her about it today . . not when she's angry. I keep it to myself, like saying a little wish for her instead.

She dresses quicker this morning than normal . . in front of the window to let the rest of the world watch if they want to.

It's just me that she wants to keep herself from.

Punishing me for the kiss I gave him last night.

"I fucking saw you," she said last night. "Don't tell me it was nothing, because I *saw it*."

Anything I said would have made it worse so I kept silent. I kept awake most of the night wondering.

She's never stayed this mad at me through the night before. I figured this would be the same but I was wrong.

I know I need to say something now. I know for certain when she doesn't ask "How do I look?" like she always does.

"What's the big deal? You kiss Kinna all the time!" I point out.

"What?" She spits it out like fire when she whips around.

I shrink under her stare as she steps away from the window . . feeling like I said the wrong thing as she gets brighter . . flooding me with the day coming in through the window . . my skin burning white . . not so much from the sun but from the red center of her eyes.

I feel myself melting the way I always do when I'm yelled at. I fold my hands under the blanket when I mumble, "You heard me. What's the big deal?"

"You don't get it!" she shouts . . twisting her face into a mean smile the way Sandra always does when she's trying to make us feel stupid about something. "There's a big fucking difference, Kid. Why don't you grow up and figure it out?"

I wipe my eyes when she goes on and says, "Maybe Kinna was right. Maybe what she told me yesterday was true . . that you're too young to be with." Now I start to cry a little because to me it sounds like I'm not worth keeping . . that like everyone else she thinks I'm only good for leaving behind. She knows this will hurt me, so it hurts even more that she'd do it.

She rubs her temples with her hands . . pulls her skin back to make her eyes small before letting them go with a sigh . . wanting something from me but I don't know what to say or do so I sit there crying. Maybe that's actually what she wants. Maybe she just wants to hurt me as much as seeing me kiss Dune hurt her.

She stops shouting when she talks again.

Still angry but a gentler kind of it.

"Kid, we're out of here in five months. Once summer comes and I'm eighteen, we're taking off." She throws her arms out to the side like soaring through time . . talking fast to make it happen quicker. "The three of us leaving all this shit behind once and for all. Remember?"

All of her dreams play out in her eyes like switching channels on the television . . all the things she wants out of life . . the cameras following her . . the limos and pent-houses . . the beach in summer with the sun like gold in the sky that we can own and all we have to do for it is sing and be beautiful.

"I remember," I whisper . . not remembering it the same as her though.

"There's no way I'm taking him with me, so you better figure out real fast who it's gonna be."

She refuses to look at me when she says it. It's the first time she's ever said anything that would break her promise of forever.

My thumb rubs the tattoo on my wrist . . trying to get warmth because the eyes feel empty and frozen.

Pausing at the door . . the sound of her breath like

someone finishing a race . . coming up behind me to put her hand on my neck . . trying to make it sound different than how she said it . . trying to make it sound like I'd be the one leaving if I didn't pick her over him . . saying, "I want you to come . . but I'm going either way."

I have to fight to get the words out . . pull them from so deep inside me that I'm afraid they won't have any sound left when they reach my tongue . . worried that once they've been said they'll be permanent . . the way clipping a bird's wings means they can never fly again.

"He needs me too."

He needs me to help him be whole again . . needs me to show him how to shine . . teach him about angels and his brother who is fine and making wishes by the river if he looks hard enough. He needs me to be with him . . to watch his back to make sure he doesn't get hurt again . . needs me at the very least not to be the one who does it to him.

She pulls her hand off me like I'm a disease . . like something contagious that burns to the touch. She slams a fist down on the bed the way my dad would bang his on the table whenever I said anything to make him mad.

But I didn't say anything wrong and I won't take it back.

"You know what? Just forget it, Kid." She moves toward the door like she has gasoline in her bloodstream. "If you want to live in some fairy tale, then fine, go ahead. Pretend he isn't going to turn into an asshole like your father and mine."

"He's different," I tell her. "He's one of us, even if he is a boy."

"You think he's going to turn into some prince just because you kissed him! Well, he's not, okay? He's not!" She's trying to make it more true the louder her words get.

I shake my head back and forth to let her know she's wrong.

She only rolls her eyes and starts in on me again.

"Wake up already! We're not some family of thieves that was somehow meant to be together. We're just a bunch of kids with shitty parents and rotten luck. You'd better figure out quick that life isn't like the stories you tell me at night. In real life, happy endings are never perfect and only come when you take them."

She opens the door and steps into the hallway. Only one last look back at me as I wipe my eyes raw and pink.

I hear the front door open. Footsteps on the porch.

I catch a glimpse of her hair against her black coat as she walks down the sidewalk. Then I pull on a pair of jeans and slip into her sneakers. I rush into the hallway because I can still catch her. I can hurry . . throw my arms around her and beg her not to be like this . . ready to promise her anything in the world if she takes it all back.

But I don't even get to the front door before Sandra gets in my way. "You don't go anywhere today," she says, her hand held like a stop sign. "You have an *appointment,* so you had better go clean up a bit. It looks like a bunch of animals live here. Tell that boy to stay here too. Get some books together and make it look like you're learning something." She finishes her thought with the spark of a lighter . . death breath of a dragon as she sits back down again.

Alexi is gone. So far away down the street, I could never catch her.

"Elizabeth, are you listening?" the social worker asks me. Her hand waves in front of my face . . bringing my eyes back from staring far away . . from looking off into the distance where the future waits like items on a rack in a department store . . so many choices as far as you can see . . and this woman would tell me I could have any of them I wanted just like all the rest like her have done before.

Seems every person has one they want for me . . all have their favorites picked out for me to wear . . dress me up in their dreams . . each of them thinking theirs will fit me the best.

Sandra has a mask knotted around my face . . two holes for my eyes . . something invisible to cover the rest of me to make it so I always get away . . but a leash around my neck so that I always come back to get put away in my place.

Alexi doesn't care what I wear as long I dress myself under a spotlight . . as long as we are dressed like twins.

No one lets me pick for myself.

No one wants what I want . . to be naked and free with butterfly wings.

The social worker is no different.

This woman's younger than the last one. They must think that'll make it easier for her to convince me . . easier for her to pretend to be my friend instead of the person assigned to my case this week.

"The hearing is a week from today. So I have to know." She grips a pen tightly between her fingers.

In her mind she picks out a future for me too . . one with a pretty dress . . ribbon around the waist that ties in the back . . bows in my hair brushed to make me look sweet . . be the perfect daughter or the perfect victim . . either way the outfit works the same.

I hear her explain both sides of everything to me again . . repeating them slower . . in shorter sentences like I couldn't understand them the first time. I either need to forgive him or I need to speak up for what he did to me . . it's my choice . . one or the other because (she says) ignoring it isn't an option . . choosing not to deal with it won't make it like it never happened.

"I did deal with it, two years ago." I raise my voice because I'm sick of all of them thinking I'm running away from something again . . because what she's saying to me is the same shit Alexi said this morning . . that I'm not grown up enough to understand.

I understand fine.

I've understood for years.

I sat there and told the world everything . . they were the ones who didn't understand . . or didn't listen because now they want to do it all over again. They're the ones pretending things never happened. Not me.

The pen drops to the table . . her hands thrown up in the air. "Fine . . fine." She's not trying to hide her annoyance. She says she'll tell them I don't wish to participate and adds that's fine with her. She just wants to make sure it's what I really want. She's seen too many kids regret it later on.

I can see into the living room when I lean back in my chair . . Dune sitting on the floor with a book open on the coffee table . . some kind of math or something . . Sandra trying to make it look like we're learning . . not caring that Dune is only scribbling pictures . . as long as it looks the way it's supposed to . . as long as the checks still come in the mail like the ones on the counter behind me.

Putting all the files back in her bag, the social worker tells me my father's going to get out. "A good record while he's been in . . no other priors . . a child who doesn't care enough to show up . . why shouldn't they let him go?"

She studies me as she says he'll probably be out before spring.

I know it's all a trick .. one of the things they're taught to get a reaction .. a chapter in their handbook on difficult orphans titled HOW TO GET THE QUIET KID TO REACT .. a set up .. like the cops who used to surround the empty buildings and round us up. They'd back us into a corner with nowhere left to run.

I know what she's trying to do but I fall for it anyway.

I can't help myself. I can't let her get away with it.

"Why are you doing this?" I yell. "Why are you making it like I don't care?" The innocent look on her face tells me she's not doing anything .. that I'm the one making it seem that way by not agreeing to go there.

Shit on that!

And shit on them too if they need me to spell it out .. if they need to hear from me that sometimes it still hurts to think about any of it.

Let them do whatever they want .. but don't dare think that I don't care.

"I just think you should reconsider," she says, cold as the wind blowing against the window.

"No," I say, shaking my head more violently this time.

No .. because everything is going wrong and I want it to stop. I want everyone to stop telling me what to do. I want to decide for myself what I want.

185

She looks at me a different way when she gets up to leave . . studying me . . searching for something wrong with me.

"Social workers are like cops for foster kids" . . that's what Alexi told me the first day I was dropped off here. She said they were always suspicious . . always looking around for anything that might not be the way it's supposed to. She said it was always better to lie . . to only tell them what they want to hear or they'll find something wrong to blame my behavior on.

I'm tired of never being allowed to feel what's inside of me . . tired of having to hide it because someone else says so.

There's whispering back and forth outside the kitchen. The social worker's talking to Sandra about me like I'm a child who doesn't know what the words they use mean. She asks if everything's okay . . if there have been any problems in the house . . if I've been acting out. She's pretending all of a sudden that they didn't just dump me here to get me out of the way . . that the system doesn't work the way it really does . . out of sight and out of mind as long as the paperwork is in order. She's pretending she actually cares how my life is going.

"You know how they get moody sometimes," Sandra says. This is bullshit. She knows as well as I do what's really going on . . and knows exactly what she needs to say and just the right way to say it . . polite with a little bit of worry sprinkled in. "This whole thing has been hard on her." I want to laugh, because she doesn't even know what the whole thing is, let alone how it's been with me.

I keep looking at Dune as they talk . . the way he looks at me . . his eyes soft like he's saying sorry . . folding his hands together like he wants to hold them over my ears so I won't have to listen to the way they talk about me.

"Perhaps she should talk to someone." The social worker says it like a warning . . saying it as she glances around . . a threat that she'll be here again and again to keep checking up if we don't listen to what she says.

Sandra says she'll talk to me but the woman says, "I mean someone like a doctor, given her family history." She sends a sideways glance at me the same as my dad's lawyer did when he spoke to the jury.

Everything inside me snaps then . . everything I was trying to hold in comes rushing out.

"So now I'm *crazy* just because I don't agree with you?" I yell. Sandra quickly puts her arm around my waist . . whispering in my ear . . telling me to let it go . . turning back to the social worker with a promise to make an appointment with the doctor at their offices.

I want to dig my fingers into the social worker's face when she smiles at me before she leaves. The smile says she wins . . that she'll always win because that's what being in foster care means. I've got no rights unless they give them to me.

"What are you trying to do . . screw everything up?" Sandra asks me as soon as the woman is gone. She pulls me back into the kitchen and forces me against the counter . . my wrists held together by her hands . . saying I'll have more to worry about than seeing some doctor if the city comes down on her . . that she'll sell me out in a heartbeat if they start snooping around.

"Don't think for a minute that you are worth a shit to me," she growls. "Now get out and do what I keep you around to do. It's the only thing you're good for."

Sunlight shines through the front window like a sea of angels has come to take me away. I head straight for them . . not even trying to make up something to say to her. I don't bother to take my coat or backpack . . I don't stop for anything. I'm only trying to get into the open air before I can't keep from crying.

SPREAD YOUR WINGS
AND FLY AWAY

Dune makes his way across the street toward the stairs of the subway where I'm shivering . . the afternoon in his hair . . blue sky with a promise of better things . . the wind making his clothes dance in the rays of the sun as he crosses the white lines painted on the asphalt.

A parade of people marches between us . . the sound of their shoes on the sidewalk . . fractions of conversations breaking apart . . an intense humming of electricity all around me like a storm made by machines.

I can't think straight. I'm drowning in sound . . wanting to sing because my song is like an air bubble to help me breathe but there's none in me.

My hands relax in my lap and I clear my throat to keep from coughing.

There's a smell of rainbows on his hands . . clean like the smell of soap when he touches me here and there like he's not sure where to put them . . finally he swings his arms to drape the coat over my body like armor to protect me from the cold . . his arm around my waist like armor made of elephant bones to protect me from being alone.

I say thanks by smiling.

"Hey . . I'm sorry," he says. "About all of that." He glances over at the corner where our so-called home is . . tracing a line in the air that keeps us attached to it . . a shorter leash than a day before . . tighter than the one that was so long I almost started to believe it wasn't there.

"It's not your fault," I say, sniffing away anything left that wants to come out.

"Yeah, I know. It's just . . I know how much it sucks sometimes."

I feel so stupid for all the things I've told him since he came here . . how great I made it seem to be one of us when really we're no better off than anywhere else we came from. It's the same shit disguised as a different story. It sounds better to tell but still ends the same way.

He knew it all along . . about Sandra . . from the very first day he knew what she was . . what we were to her.

I can't help it . . can't stop hoping that wishes aren't just worthless scraps of paper that turn to wet tissue as soon as they hit the water. If I start thinking that way, what's the point? What is there to ever make me think anything will get better?

"Dune, do you think they're right . . that there's something wrong with me?" I ask him because I don't know anymore. Maybe I am just hiding from everything in the world. Maybe they really are the ones who've got it all figured out. Maybe I'm just like my mom. Maybe I am crazy too.

"I don't know," he says . . watching a group of people squeeze by us on their way up to the platform . . not really watching them just looking . . thinking about the question some more before finishing. "But I don't think anyone else knows either."

I turn my head and see him in full color, with the world dim behind him. I see what I wasn't able to describe to Alexi before: I need him as much as I thought he needed me.

It's like he knows too. He helps me up . . knowing without me having to tell him that I want to get out of here . . that I need to get far away . . as far as the subway can take us as we climb up the stairs.

"C'mon, let's go," he says . . and I can feel the way his arms hold me up . . hold me against him . . the rush of the train like the rush of a speeding car . . leading me away from my life like pulling me out of the way before it kills me.

Forever doesn't matter as much as today. Fuck forever because it's too much to think about all the time. Worrying about forever ruins everything.

"I'm glad I met you," I say . . bringing my face to his . . smiling for the first time all day when I leave my kiss on him like making a new color in a rainbow. The train blowing past the buildings so fast that they crumble into space and leave nothing in the world but us.

That's fine with me. Because that's how it feels falling in love. It feels like flying off the end of the world where wishes fall from the sky like shooting stars . . leaving all that other stuff behind . . ready to leave it back there forever because it doesn't matter to me as long as we're together.

From the platform we can see out to the canal broken by the splash of raindrops . . the highway overpass in the distance where the cars slow to the stop of traffic. Between them both is the place I wanted to show him . . a forgotten stretch of Brooklyn where the grass grows wild.

I say "C'mon" and pull him past the vending machines, through the turnstile, and down the stairs through a fragmented crowd of people. As we move onto the sidewalk, the rain begins to fall harder on our heads. Our hair sticks to our faces and the back of our necks.

He doesn't ask where I'm taking him. I pull him along Smith Street, then down the next street that doesn't have a name. There's no sign telling it anyways. It doesn't lead anywhere except to the fence.

Just behind the last building there's a place where the

wire has been cut . . an opening in the fence big enough for us to slip in.

I know it will still be there . . even though I haven't been back here in so long . . because the lost corners of the city never change . . the places nobody knows exist . . the secret parts that are like paradise for us to trespass . . wastelands set aside for souls with nowhere else to go . . forgotten just like us.

I hook my fingers over the rusted metal and hesitate for a second on purpose . . hesitate before peeling back the wire to make a gate for us to crawl through.

It opens just like I remember.

I lean my body against the fence to clear a space for him to go in. The smell of the canal is like the smell of rain. The tall grass on the other side is like a hidden forest protected from the rest of the world.

"What is this place?" he asks. The brown of his eyes looking brighter against the gray sky . . like the center of a flower or the inside of a heart.

"It's where I used to live," I tell him as his hands take my place from the inside and I slide under the sharp edges of our entrance. My shoes sinking in the soft dirt as soon as the concrete ends. "Wanna see?" It's not really a question . . more of an invitation, I guess.

In between drops of rain, he nods. Our feet step in

between broken bottles littering the path with tiny slivers of glass.

There's a rare sound of thunder in the winter afternoon and I tell him to hurry up as I start to run. I scream with laughter as the sky explodes down on us . . the ground turning to mud. I leave him behind as I race for the shelter of the highway held high above us by tall pillars of concrete.

Little streams spill over the road four stories above . . a curtain made of heaven . . a waterfall of good luck smiling at us . . each drop like a tiny kiss on our heads . . salty like the taste of tears when I lick my lips and show him the burned-out skeleton of a car tucked away like a bird's nest between two towers. The tall grass behind it has kept it hidden well enough that it's stayed in its place since the last night I slept in it.

I climb in where the door is supposed to be . . pushing my way into the backseat . . sinking in lower than the missing windows.

I hear the pigeons dance on the roof as Dune climbs in next to me . . the tap-tapping of their feet like the sound of the rain sweeping over the road. The pigeons don't seem to mind us being like one of them for a little while . . nesting to get out of the storm.

"How'd you ever find this place?" He sounds like we've discovered a deserted island . . the broken dials on the dashboard like the wreck of our ship . . the murky water in the canal like the far reaches of a dirty ocean.

"By accident, I guess. It sort of found me." I put my hands up to my mouth . . remembering the way it was like following shooting stars . . the blinking lights of a radio tower through the dark . . singing softly the sound it made to watch . . singing "on then off" down an empty street where the sidewalk came to an end.

It's how I've found every place I ever stayed . . drifting through the city . . letting go . . letting the part of me that's closer to the angels guide me through . . trusting it to leave me in a safe place.

I smile to myself . . remembering how I used to drive Gretchen crazy sometimes when we would search for a new empty building to live in . . how I would stomp my foot and simply say no because I didn't know how else to describe to her that it didn't feel right. She would look at me . . take a deep breath . . then we'd move on to another place.

"Dune?" I say . . watching as his hand traces the stitches in the seat's fabric . . tilting my head back to look at him . . the wind catching his hair on top and making it stand on end. "Do you ever think that . . I don't know . . that you're missed?"

"By my parents, you mean?" He gives his answer in the tone of his voice . . the way he says "parents" like they are imaginary.

I tell him not only them . . but friends maybe.

"I don't know. Maybe, I guess. I didn't have very many friends. My brother was my best friend, you know. He's the only one who'd miss me. If he could, I mean."

I fold my arms around his waist . . bury my cheek against his coat and whisper a song like a little bird.

His body shakes beneath me . . rapid beat of his heart with the rise and fall of his chest . . and I'm so sure he's starting to cry until I see he's laughing . . a surprise smile on his face breaking up the sadness the way the sun will break up the clouds in the morning.

"You know what I can't stop thinking about?" he asks, brushing the hair away from his face and holding it against the wind. "Soon as we got here . . I haven't been able to stop thinking how much he'd love this place."

I share the smile with him when he tells me stories about forts they built in the woods behind their house . . playing games from their favorite TV shows . . playing characters from their favorite stories. We both laugh when he tells me which parts he played . . picturing him as a cowboy with a swing set for a horse . . as a space explorer with the spokes of bike wheels like the roaring of a jet engine.

I tell him the stories I used to make up in my bed-room . . draping the lace curtain from the window over my head like a veil . . marrying my stuffed animals one by one. I'd be a princess for each of them . . our castle would be made of pink clouds and all of them would be able to talk and move on their own.

As we share our stories back and forth, the rain gives way to the night. Eventually our voices grow weak from the cold . . scratching out the last syllables until there are no more words . . our fingers locked together to keep warm . . staring at each other's smiles until our eyes grow tired too.

I know now why I brought us here . . leading us here like a wolf following the cry of other wolves toward the warmth of the den. It's all clear to me as I look at the tag Dune has drawn on the seat . . a mask like the one that binds us together.

We were brought here to steal our lives back . . steal our memories back . . steal the future and make it ours.

That's how it feels anyway . . being this close to him . . our hearts side by side as we quit trying to stay awake. It feels more like healing than running away.

NEVER GO WITHOUT
SAYING GOOD-BYE

The city always looks dirtier in the morning than at night. The sun creeps into every crack to show all the places that aren't perfect. All the boarded up windows . . all the dented cars . . all the trash littering the gutters as I step into a new day that always smells like coffee and gasoline.

"You sure you want to do this?" Dune asks . . not trying to talk me out of anything . . just making sure I know what I'm getting into.

I do.

I'm pretty sure anyway of what is going to happen when we get to Kinna's. I'm pretty sure it's not going to be happy like birthday parties are or anything like that. But I have to go through with it anyways. Even if she tells me she hates me forever, that's okay. I just need her to know that I don't hate her.

I can't leave things with Alexi the way they got left with Gretchen. I don't want to be wondering years from now if there was something I could have done . . some way to keep her my friend.

Friends stop sharing the same dream at some point. They drift in different directions. Like the friends I used to have living on the street . . a lot of them drifted back home . . some drifted into juvenile detention . . others are still out there searching for something to dream about.

My dream was never the same as Alexi's. Mine was just to be with her. Not because I want all the things she wants, like being famous and rich. I just wanted someone to hold onto me if the angels dropped from the sky to take me away. I wanted her next to me in the dark, whispering for them please not to take me the way my mother always did.

But that was before . . that's when I was still scared of everything . . before she taught me not be afraid of the world . . to own it with a smile . . to make it mine . . make it however I want it to be. Only I don't think either of us thought that once I did decide what I wanted, she wouldn't be the star in the sky that made me warmest.

"How do you know she's even going to be here?" he asks when I point out which building is Kinna's. Twenty-eight stories tall . . thirty-two apartments to every floor . . perfect view of a dead end area of Queens from every window high enough to be clear of the buildings on either side of the street.

"I just do," I say. I know she's with Kinna the same way she knows I'm with him if I'm not with her.

I don't notice how frozen my hands and feet are until we step inside the first doors where the buzzers are. The heater blows down on us . . my hands so cold that it hurts trying to get them warm . . my skin pink like flowers bitten by frost.

I rub my hands together to get a sense of feeling back . . cup my palms and blow into the bowl they make as I scan the numbers for the one that will connect me to where Alexi is. When I find it, I bite down on my finger before I finally push.

It feels like forever comes and goes before the static comes alive and I hear Kinna's voice saying, "Yeah? Who's there?"

"It's me . . it's Kid." I can hear her hand lift off the button that lets me listen into her apartment . . cutting me off so I can't hear what they say about me . . what they decide. I push the button again and talk. "Please let me up," I say.

There's no reply on the other end . . just the click of the lock releasing to open the door.

We shuffle through. The wet soles of our shoes squeak across the floor, leaving footprints made of mud for anyone to follow our steps as we get on the elevator. The whole ride up to the seventeenth floor, I wonder what I'm going to say.

There's a quick whiff of fried food and cinnamon when the doors open to let us off.

The lights never work and we have to make our way mostly in the dark.

The door to Kinna's is open just a crack. Her face is like a shadow when she steps into view . . a small rectangle of her . . the skin around her eyes painted purple like the sunrise on another planet . . the corner of her mouth cut in half by the chain locking the door to the wall.

I don't have to see Alexi to know exactly what she's doing . . that she's grabbing at the ends of her hair . . telling Kinna she doesn't want to see me . . Kinna saying "Maybe you should go, Kiddo" with the slow way she has of slurring her words when her head moves side to side.

"Please let me talk to her," I say. Then we both listen and hear only silence, so she unhooks the lock and steps aside to let the door swing open.

"Be my guest," she says. "It'll give me a break from listening to her bitch."

Kinna and Dune stay in the living room while I go to the bedroom. The stereo. is turned up loud enough to give us privacy. It doesn't make it any easier to speak though.

"So what?" she says. "You came here to break up with

me or something?" Acting like she doesn't care when she says it . . pacing around in front of the window on the other side of the room.

I stay close to the door . . my hands behind my back . . fingertips resting on the handle.

"No. I don't know." I'm thinking maybe it was a mistake to come here after all.

We both stare at the winter sky outside the window . . different from any other season . . like the blue has worn thin . . the shell of an egg too easy to break to keep alive all the things growing inside it.

I come away from the door . . toward Alexi with her back turned to me. Her hands covering her eyes . . mine folded behind me . . I'm wondering if the distance has any way of bringing us closer when I whisper, "I just don't want you to hate me."

"I don't hate you," she says. There's something in her voice sadder than hate . . the song of something beautiful dying.

I feel her whole body flinch when I reach out to put my hands on her head. I run my fingers through her hair to make her strong, the way she's always done with me. I'm showing her how much she'll always mean to me no matter what happens today or tomorrow or any day after.

We hold each other at a safe distance when she turns around. Our hands rest on each other's elbows like dancers in the old movies we used to watch together late at night. We know we'll have to separate once the music ends.

She tells me she was worried about me by petting me behind the ear . . fixing the knots in my hair as she asks me if I slept outside . . saying I look it when I say we did.

"You can't go back to Sandra," she says.

"I know," I tell her. "I never would anyways."

Fuck Sandra.

I'm worth more than she thinks I am . . worth more than what she uses me for.

"They're going to be looking for you," she says. "Sandra called the police last night when you didn't come back." Then she tells me everything Sandra told them . . how she pretended to be worried that I'd hurt myself . . how I hadn't been myself lately and she was afraid I was going to do something crazy . . afraid that Dune was going to make me do something crazy because she told the cops he was the cause of everything.

"Did you tell them it wasn't true?" I ask, a lump in my throat making it hard to swallow.

The tears in her eyes are answer enough. "I'm sorry," she says. "I went along with it. I had to."

I feel the rush of panic like fire in me. We've got to get out of the city . . we have to go now . . before they find us . . past the borders where maybe somebody might believe us if we ever got caught.

Alexi says she didn't know what happened until after . . not until Sandra said if she ever got me back she was sure my dad would pay a lot of money to find out where I was. Before that, she thought Sandra might actually let me stay again . . and once Dune was gone everything would go back to being like it was.

My bones are like buildings falling to the ground when she grabs me, saying, "I swear I didn't know."

Her eyes are wet against the back of my neck . . her words muffled against my spine.

"I'll be fine," I whisper.

My butterfly wings have grown in . . strong enough to carry me off . . beautiful enough to protect me.

I can almost see them when I catch my reflection in the window . . transparent rainbows wide enough to cover all of Queens.

It's almost like she can see it too because she lets go. She takes her hands away like I'm her little bird learning to be on my own . . setting me free into the world . . watching me walk out of the room like watching me flying toward the sun.

Dune's sitting nervous on the sofa, his leg tapping faster than the music. His glance catches me and I can tell by the way he springs up that Kinna let him know everything that Alexi just told me.

"C'mon, we gotta go," I say. I take his hand and pull

him closer to the door before Kinna stops me . . hands me money folded up like wishes ready to be made.

"You gonna need this," she says. She tells us not to take the bus or the trains out of Manhattan . . says if they're really looking at all they'll be looking there. "Take the PATH train to Jersey," she advises. "Then go wherever you know."

"Thanks." I'm mouthing it more than saying it since the sound doesn't really come out . . everything seems too heavy to speak.

Kinna leans in close to me . . the smell of kiwi on her breath when she whispers, "It's from her" . . looking over in the direction of Alexi . . so skinny that she's starting to fade from view.

Before I leave I go back over to her . . press our wrists together . . make us Siamese and feel the itch on my skin of knowing I'll see her again someday . . that we are sisters forever . . because it can never wash away.

Nothing left to be said.

A quick wave is all that's left when the elevator door closes.

SHOPPING MALL MIRACLES

The sound of the highway is soothing as we look up at the streetlight a little ways away. I pretend it's a star looking down on us and I fold my hands like making a wish . . asking only for it to keep giving us good luck like we've had since we left the city six days ago.

I've lost track of where we are . . which mall is which as we've made our way from one to the other like connecting dots to dots on a map. We live in the malls during the day and find hiding places around their parking lots to sleep at night.

"I like this one. Maybe we can stay a few more days here," I say as we snuggle in closer to each other, sharing a sleeping bag we paid for the first night.

"Sure." Dune rubs his hands together when the wind finds its way down into the storm ditch where we've made a little camp.

It's only the second night we've stayed here . . but one night was all it took to know it was better than the last place we slept . . a little alley behind the last mall a few towns away. I couldn't sleep there. I kept waking up worried that someone was going to come walking through with a flashlight like the cops always did when I slept in abandoned buildings . . search and destroy like exterminators hunting bugs living behind in the walls.

Here in the storm drain is better. No one can see it . . probably no one knows it's here. I checked this morning . . walked all around above checking for any signs of it. The grass between the highway and the parking lot looked flat . . it's hard to tell that it dips down in the middle . . not unless you go looking. *The Grande Mall Canyon* . . that's what I named it.

The entrance to the drain is wide too . . dry without any rain for a week or so . . perfect for us to hide in at night and watch the streetlights twinkle as planes leave trails of light through the fog.

Dune drew a mask on the concrete by our heads . . marking it as ours . . BEWARE OF DOGS for anyone who stumbles on us. We'll bite to keep ourselves safe if we have to.

I feel around in the sleeping bag for part of him to grab onto . . my hand crawling over his stomach like a spider until he starts laughing . . tickling him until we both roll

214

over, out of breath. And I lie perfectly still as his arms close around me . . his hands locking together behind the small of my back . . resting my head on his shoulder and happy just to have him hold me.

Twelve lanes of cars roar by above the grass . . gasoline music and the scream of sirens now and then. But even with all their noise we are by ourselves. Looking up at the clouds moving fast across the sky like giant birds in a war . . watching them erase the moon and knowing that I'm happier than I've ever been in my life, lying here as the first flakes of snow begin to fall inches from our sleeping bag.

"Are you happy too?" I ask him. "Happy like I am." I lift my chin up to see him half lit in the shadows. It's enough for me to see him smile . . enough to show me his answer.

He starts to talk . . then stops and stares up at the street-light like he's searching for words floating in the electricity.

When I touch his face it feels like porcelain. It's smooth like one of the dolls I used to take to bed with me. There's nothing rough about him . . nothing mean like most boys I've known.

"I never thought I'd meet anybody like you," he says.

"There is nobody like me," I say, getting him to smile and forget about before.

Every day since we left has felt like the beginning of a new life. There's nothing we can't say to each other . .

nothing we can't share that the other won't understand . . not like me and Alexi . . how one of us had to shine brighter. With Dune it's different . . like two stars so close together that they shine as one.

Here in the dark under the lights of the parking lot, he says, "I love you, Kid."

It sounds like a song . . like the only sound in the world.

It will last forever inside me . . long after every building rusts and turns to sand it will still be there . . because his words become permanent when I crawl over him. Let our breath mix and become one before joining the clouds.

I make him say it again when I open my mouth . . "I love you" . . swallowing each syllable when we kiss . . keep them like a tattoo that only shows on the inside of my skin.

I open my eyes just in time to see the sky begin to break apart . . the clouds shattering like glass and sprinkling soft pieces down to the ground.

I pull Dune up as quick as I can. I don't even bother to put on my shoes as I rush up the hill in my bare feet. My toes barely touch the frozen ground as the snow begins to fall faster.

I twirl around with my arms out . . around and around at circus speed as the blacktop of the parking lot is erased and the storm makes the world blank again. I'm waiting for a new wish to be written everywhere I can see.

I grab onto his arms and make him spin around with me . . make him listen to the song made by the traffic as the tires start to splash on the wet pavement . . make him catch me when I grow too dizzy and start to fall.

The words feel strange coming out of my mouth. I've never had much practice saying them. Only in whispers. Only to myself and never aloud. It's a new feeling on my tongue like the new feeling in my heart.

"I love you too," I say as we fall softly to the ground like snowflakes.

PARANOID SECURITY

The inside of the mall is like Broadway downtown only with a roof over it and lots of benches everywhere to sit on. It's the same store names over each door and the same collection of people too . . like the rest of the world is populated by scooping up part of the crowds in New York and placing them randomly in malls across the world.

Dune laughs when I tell him that . . when I point out each person who passes where we sit. I make up where I've seen them before . . "59th Street coming out of the supermarket under the bridge" . . "Always . . I *always* see her on Astor Place" . . "I think he works at the deli by the subway stop near Sandra's" . . laughing harder each time because it seems to get more true . . like suddenly the mall is just a miniature model of the city.

Everyone just takes up the same roles wherever they go.

We're no different, I guess. We fade into the scenery . . an invisible invasion that comes one day and is gone the next. We're perfectly anonymous like any other kid hanging out here.

Security guards are the only ones we have to watch out for. Because of them, we have to make sure we move around every hour or so. Otherwise they start to harass us with wheres and whys.

We usually spot them before they spot us . . get up casually . . carrying a bag from a store to make it look like we bought something. If you act naturally, they take no notice.

Play innocent and they assume you are.

In a couple more days though, even that won't work. We'll get too familiar. We'll have to move to someplace else.

"Let's head over to the food court," Dune says, nodding at one of them coming around the corner. They're easy to spot with their white shirts and radios on their shoulders.

He spots us just as easily too . . teens with dirty eyes during the day . . the time of day we're supposed to be shut away in a school somewhere. People notice that more outside the city.

The shopping bag falls on the floor when I stand up. Sunglasses slide across the tile. It's too thin a crowd to keep it quiet. Eyes dart to me like spotting a mouse running through a kitchen.

I get nervous when the guard starts coming toward us . . the click of his heavy shoes . . the rattle of keys against his leg.

Dune bends down quick to pick up the bag. He grabs my hand away from my mouth and walks me away without a word because we both saw the guard giving a long glance at us . . something in his eyes . . too much like a clerk in a store who knows you're there to steal.

We walk away like we belong here the same as everyone else. I glance back as Dune puts his arm around me . . I get a peek before I kiss the side of his face and it looks like the coast is clear.

"Is he watching us?" Dune asks.

I shake my head. "Nope. We're free." I run up to the fountain with a large elephant statue spraying water over its back. There's a fake plastic jungle on an island in the center. Pennies cover the bottom like copper-colored sea shells.

All the wishes sparkle as the sun shines through the glass roof above me . . a treasure of good things waiting to come true.

I never liked making wishes in fountains too much. It takes longer for them to come true . . at least that's what I always thought when I was little. My mother said those wishes had to wait their turn . . sit there and rust until the fountain emptied its water into the ocean . . that it could take days or even years . . that only the fountain could tell when it was full.

I never wished for anything big or important in a fountain.

Now I dig through my pocket and pull out a quarter. I close it tight in my hands until my palms get sweaty. I figure without the river close by I'll have to get used to fountains . . even for important things.

I toss the coin in the air.

"What'd you wish for?" Dune asks when I come back to where he's standing.

I frown and make a face at him. He laughs and says, "I know, I know," because everybody knows nothing comes true once you tell.

It was nothing much anyways . . nothing he'd care about.

It's just something stupid . . wishing Alexi is as happy wherever she goes as I am right now. "C'mon," I say, "I thought you were hungry."

"I am." He puts his hand over his stomach and pretends to growl, trying to get me to smile. But he doesn't even have to try. I'm smiling anyways.

The tables are spread out all over like people waiting for

the train at rush hour. Most of them are empty . . it's a weekday and too early for lunch, really.

There's every kind of food to choose from but only for those willing to pay. We're not looking to waste money on any of it though. Not when all we have to do is find some-one around our age working at one of them . . talk to them a bit and see what they can give us for free.

Usually this time of day when it's slow, they can give us anything we ask for.

We make a quick circle around . . checking the faces . . checking for someone who might not be so strict about their job.

"That's the girl who made us sandwiches the other day," I say, pointing over where the girl is leaning against the counter . . waiting for her to see us and wave.

She waves back and that's all we need to get us over there.

"Hey . . you guys are still around," she says. We nod and tell her we're probably leaving soon.

We tell everybody the same story so we don't get con-fused. We tell them we're cousins . . that we're traveling around . . taking a year off before college. Most of them look at me and don't believe us. I look too young . . Dune does too . . but most of them let it go because it's none of their business. And besides, we're good enough liars that they can't be sure since we say it like we mean it. We bring it up only in pieces so it's not like making up a whole story all at once.

"We're just sticking around, you know. Visiting people," I say.

I see our reflection in the mirror behind her . . the way both of us are starting to look a little like me and Gretchen used to . . a week without a real shower and my hair is a little too greasy beneath my hat . . too many knots to pull out . . too much dirt under both of our fingernails . . a stain around our eyes . . stains on our clothes that are starting to show how we haven't taken them off . . the look of a storm drain on the sleeves.

She notices it too . . the smell of homelessness on us like the smell of smoke on Sandra. Even though we use the mall bathrooms to wash up, it's not the same.

"Look," she says, "it's okay. You don't have to tell me, since it's none of my business. I just like the company, that's all. It's boring as shit working here." We share smiles like promising to keep a secret.

"Thanks," I whisper as she offers to make each of us something to eat.

I'm about to tell her what I want when she looks over my head and says, "Shit . . it's Tim." I follow in the mirror to see where she's looking . . across the tables to the beginning of the food court . . the same security guard who saw us before.

The sandwich girl tells us, "He's a real hard ass about us giving away food. Come back in twenty minutes, okay? I'll make something for you guys to take." She gives me a wink the way Alexi always did. I smile and mumble "okay," hoping she doesn't hear my stomach rumbling as we walk away.

I keep looking back to make sure he's not following us . . hold my breath until I see him turn and walk the other way . . disappearing back to the part of the mall we came from.

"We can wait in here," I say, ducking into the bookstore to search through the racks of magazines until it's safe to go back. We'll get our food and get out of here . . hang out in our canyon just until later when the shifts change . . come back after the sun sets . . after the crowds look more like us once school's let out.

Dune flips through the music magazines . . looking at the pictures mostly . . pretending to be interested more than he is . . pretending not to be starving.

I reach for one of the fashion magazines. The girl on the cover is like a beautiful bird to be watched gliding through the clouds. I start wondering about me . . if I'm as pretty as she is.

I'm about to ask Dune . . about to make him tell me I'm prettier . . when the photograph on the cover of the newspaper catches the corner of my eye. It's a picture of my dad . . and a picture of me as a child.

227

It feels like a fever rushes all over my skin when I pick up the paper . . fire bugs crawling over me. My vision goes all blurry . . the printing melting away under my fingers . . the ink rubbing off on my hands.

I read about my life like it's someone else's. I can't concentrate enough to read every word but I read enough to figure out that we're not as invisible as I thought . . that we're in trouble if we stay here . . that we need to go as far as possible as quick as we can.

"Let's go, Dune," I whisper. "Let's go now." I fold the paper and put it back where it came from. I check around . . by the cash register . . outside the store . . everywhere because it feels like everyone is watching me . . their eyes like cameras remembering every detail about what we're wearing to report it back to the people looking for us.

"Look at this guy," Dune says, still staring at a magazine until I step up next to him and close it. I whisper for him to put it down and come with me now, not giving him a chance to ask anything when he looks me in the eyes.

"It's not enough is it?" I ask. I'm watching Dune count the money we have and keep looking back to see if anyone is coming.

We've got less than fifty dollars . . not even close to being able to get a bus far enough to where no one will have heard about us.

"What are we gonna do, Kid?" Dune says . . running his hand through his hair and holding it there as he thinks . . scrambling for anything . . any way out of the mess we're in.

The article gave the name of Dune's old town though . . said the cops thought we might be there . . that our descriptions were sent along to the local police in that area . . asking them to distribute the information to any place we might be. This means malls and train stations. This means we have to get moving or get caught.

It's because of my dad that it made a small spot on the cover of the paper . . because his parole hearing is today . . makes it more interesting I guess . . since he's rich and I'm lost . . the timing giving them a lot to lie about.

"So many unanswered questions into the disappearance of three foster children in Queens" is how they put it . . making stories up to guess at the answers themselves . . guessing whether we are alive or dead . . if maybe my dad was involved . . if I'm together with Dune or did he take me.

I feel trapped thinking about it . . looking up and down the narrow hallway where the bathrooms are . . where we're huddled like animals cornered in an ally.

"We'll have to steal it," I say.

"There's not enough people around. We'll get caught," Dune says. He repeats all the reasons I gave him for not stealing in every other mall . . no easy getaway like in the city . . not as many places to blend in . . no way of getting miles just by running down the stairs and standing clear of closing doors.

"You're right," I say. "I know you are but I . . I just . ." I don't know if I want to scream or break down crying . . because it just all seems so unfair that any time anything good happens to me it gets taken away.

Dune comes over to me and holds me close to him. His words are warm in my ear when he tells me "don't worry" over and over until I start to relax. That's when I know how much he's changed since we first met . . no longer the scared puppy following at my feet . . more like a prince when I kiss him . . dirty clothes more like shining armor when he says, "We'll be fine."

"We can look through the cars," he tells me. "Sometimes people leave them unlocked. We found money like that all the time growing up. We only need a little more to get us to Philadelphia. There it'll be easy for us to steal a few wallets and get enough to go somewhere warmer where we can be outside all day."

We hear the sound of someone approaching at the end of the hall . . a shadow cutting in our sight.

It could be anyone but it could be the security guard who I'm convinced knows who we are.

Behind us is a fire exit that will sound an alarm if we leave through it. We decide to wait in the bathroom instead.

I follow Dune into the men's room. There's no way we're splitting up now.

We listen at the door as the footsteps get closer . . like lonely thunder on a clear sky . . a storm moving so fast that it only gives short warning. It's not him though . . no jingle of the keys and I know for sure it's not him and let Dune know . . tell him I'll wait in one of stalls in case they come in here . . or until they pass. Then we can get out.

I click the latch shut and place my feet to look like I'm going . . trying not to make a sound so that I can hear . . hearing only the sound of my heart and the faucet where Dune is washing his hands.

He clears his throat when the stranger walks in. No words are said and I know that means everything is okay. I wait another second or two, open the stall, and step out to see the man with his back turned to use the urinal on the wall.

Dune waves for me to go out . . waving toward the door and I look back at the guy . . the gray hair and nice coat . . black polished shoes and I know what Dune is trying to tell me. We've met the perfect target.

I shake my head though . . mouth to him to come with me. Nothing's changed from a minute ago. There's still no place for us to run to.

"Go," he mouths to me . . crossing his fingers and holding them up in the mirror to show me.

I show him my hands folded like a prayer.

No choice anymore as the guy begins to finish up . . reaching for the handle to flush and I need to leave before he sees me.

The world slows down as my heart speeds up.

I try to find a song inside me that will make me calm . . try to find the sound of the river somewhere in the electric hum of the hand dryer on the other side of the wall I lean against . . let out a soft sound that seems to grow louder as it bounces off the tiled floor . . against the tiled walls . . surrounding me like a wind ready to lift my wings off the ground when it's time.

Holding my breath until he comes out of there.

A rainbow shines around him like a halo when he comes up beside me . . flash of leather in his hand before it disappears in his jacket . . a quick smile to tell me there was nothing to be worried about . . all went as easy as anything.

My hands in his pockets and his wrapped around mine as we walk with our heads turned to look at each other . . ready to become ghosts forever . . ready to be forgotten by every person in the city one by one . . ready to give them all a wave good-bye as we follow the beat of our sneakers to the far end of the world.

Not fast enough though.

Not far enough when he steps into view . . parks himself at the end of the hall with eyes like headlights . . spark of violence when he speaks . . telling us to "get over here" . . a motion of his hand like whistling dogs to climb into a kennel.

Behind us the guy is coming out of the bathroom with a hand patting for his wallet.

We turn and dash to the fire exit. The guard shouts "STOP." We push past the older man who is too confused to do anything but stare with his mouth open trying to find something to say.

Cold feel of metal on my palms.

Fresh breeze falling from the sky.

Nothing between us and the horizon except parked cars.

Static on the radio behind us . . the man shouting into the receiver on his shoulder . . sound of sirens screaming somewhere in the distance.

"Don't stop," Dune says . . his eyes larger than the sun when he looks back at me . . leading the way like the howl of lost wolves in the wind.

"Once we get off the mall lot they can't do anything," he says.

We cut through row after row of dead cars parked neatly together like a graveyard . . making it harder for the patrol cars to steer around to capture us . . ducking down to keep from being seen.

The scenery begins to run together when I start to cry . . the colors of the cars all mixing like the rainbow under his skin that's not going to be able to keep us safe . . not this time and I know it . . and I know that my wings won't carry us away either . . that we're not invincible at all . . that we really are as delicate as we look.

I can't run anymore.

A sudden pain in my side . . sudden hole in my heart that makes me throw my arms down and sob . . crying like I never did before . . not even all those times hiding under my bed as a kid . . not ever when I'd been left behind . . because this is different . . this is everything we want being taken away from us.

Dune tries to get my attention . . shaking me a little . . saying how he promised me . . how he's not going to give up and that we've almost made it . . dragging me along as I fight him . . feeling too weak to take another step as they begin to close in.

I don't see it coming until it happens.

He doesn't see it coming because his eyes stay on me.

The driver doesn't see him coming until he steps in the way . . until his legs leave the ground, lifting his body in the air and setting it down a few feet away before the screech of brakes shatters my voice into a million fragments when I scream.

I stop breathing until he opens his eyes again.

I rush over to him and hold his head in my hands. He whispers with a spot of blood between his teeth as I brush his hair flat with the sweat from my palms.

The woman from the car is saying over and over how she didn't see him . . that he just rushed out in front of her . . pacing back and forth and holding her hands up in the air for the sirens to come rescue her.

The march of an army moving toward us . . the running rhythm of boots and walkie-talkies.

I rest his head in my lap and raise my arms to my side . . squint my eyes up at the sky . . my hands feeling for any sign of butterfly wings . . feel for anything as I begin to feel like I'm falling up to heaven.

Rising with him with me.

The clouds swirling so fast and the sky filled with a blazing color like the white center of the sun . . like the brightest star falling toward the ground.

And I see them.

See them the way she always told me I would . . the sky split open down the middle for them to ride stars close enough to take me away . . wings covering the sky . . smiling and laughing with their small blue hands petting the hands of the one beside them.

Spiraling faster and faster with the flutter of a storm born in heaven . . their eyes twinkling like the coins in the bottom of mall fountains . . their hands letting go of each other and reaching out for me.

The air turns my skin to snow and my bones to ice and I'm ready to go with them . . each of them perfect . . breakable to touch and I know now that she was right all along . . that I'm one of them and always have been.

I close my eyes and wait for the stars to carry us off like fireflies . . whispering to Dune in the voice of a ghost . . whispering that we finally made it to a place where forever comes to stay.

THE EVER AFTER

"Are you listening to me, Elizabeth?" She's slightly annoyed at me for staring out the window. The light coming through is tinted green from new leaves growing on the branches.

The smell of spring is like the smell of baby powder . . it makes me smile when the tiny hairs on my arm tingle. It's a little message from the wind to remind me of her . . to let me know she's fine wherever she is . . that she's burning as bright as she can.

"Hello . . this is very important." She's tapping her hand on my elbow and I roll over on my bed to look at her instead of the window. She shakes her head and smiles back at me. "Always walking through a daydream," she says, and I tell her I like when she puts it like that . . when she calls the strange things I believe in daydreams.

I fold my arms to make a pillow . . my hair draping over my skin like midnight falling over snow . . clean smell of shampoo when I breathe . . sour scent of sleep on the bed-spread the color of my lips.

If I close my eyes just right she fades into the wall behind her . . the butterfly wings I painted there become hers. I want to tell her but I keep it to myself. She'd only say I wasn't paying attention to her anyways.

It's not really true though. I am paying attention. Only I'm paying attention to things she's told me before instead of what she's telling me now . . hearing the things she said when I first came to live here . . about how I should capture what I see inside me . . let everybody see the pretty things I have to share.

At school they all say I'm really good . . at painting and stuff like that. My teachers say I'll be able to get into a college no problem . . any top art school in the city will take me. I tell them it's still too far away for me to think about. Three years is too far away when you've just been born in a new life for a few months.

Plus I'm not sure I ever want to go back to the city. There are too many places to remind me of too many things that I'm trying to forget.

"Now when we get there, they're going to ask you a lot of questions before anything else happens, okay?" She's talking slower than she normally does, either because she wants to show how important it is or because she can tell I'm still only halfway here and halfway lost in my thoughts.

"I know . . I know." I whine at her to stop. I know how it works, especially after going through all the meetings and procedures and everything involved after we got caught. I know all about questions and how to answer them.

Everyone had questions for us when we transferred back to the city.

The police had questions about where we'd been . . about why we ran away . . about the tattoos on our wrists that matched the ones of a hundred other people whose photographs they showed us . . asking if we'd seen any of them . . knew any of them . . if we even knew that the tattoos meant we belonged to them . . to a gang of thieves dating back hundreds of years.

They wanted to know where Sandra was . . if Alexi was with her . . if we had any idea where either of them would be because the list of questions for them was just as long.

Most of Child Services' questions were all about why . . why we didn't tell them what was going on . . why we didn't ask for help . . trying to blame us because everyone in the city was blaming them.

The reporters blamed them . . and they had their questions too once the story came out . . waiting with cameras outside each hearing . . putting us on the news every night for weeks as they talked about everything that was wrong with the foster care system.

Another set of questions isn't going to bother me.

"I'll be fine," I say, and Audrey smiles. She says she knows I will . . that I'm the bravest girl she's ever met. Sometimes I wonder which of us is the guardian and which is the foster child when she gets like this, wiping her eyes with the end of her sleeve.

That's what I like about her.

I'm glad they put us with her . . both of us.

It was because of all the news and everything that Dune and I got to stay together . . giving a us a little something back for the way the system let us down. It was because we were caught in New Jersey that we got to choose to come back. And I'm glad for all of it because otherwise we never would've been put with Audrey.

She never tries to act like a parent or anything . . more like a big sister that's been left in charge. That's just fine with me.

"I'll be right there with you, so if it gets too hard you let me know. Dune will be waiting too. We'll both be there for you," she says. I want her to stop worrying so much about it. I'm not scared . . I'm more nervous than any-thing . . my stomach jumping around so much that I can't eat.

The room fills with light as the clouds clear the sun, painting the walls golden.

My eyes follow the rays as they make their way across

the ceiling . . down the wall where the door is open to the hallway . . onto the carpet making its way back toward me . . over the clothes strewn all over . . past the books open to homework that can wait for another day . . and past the latest letter my dad has sent me trying to explain all the mistakes he's made. Though I'm not ready to forgive him yet, at least I'm ready to listen. Audrey says that's all anyone can ask.

"I'll give you a minute alone," she says, telling me we'll leave whenever I'm ready. She says to take however long I need . . closing the door to my room behind her as she leaves . . open just a crack for if I call for her.

My mom always said that what happens to us happens for a reason . . that we all end up where we are meant to be . . but that sometimes it's hard to see where we're going so it takes some of us longer to get there. It takes some wandering around in circles before we find the end.

Only she always thought we found the end after we died . . and that's what made it hard for her to find her way . . that was the sickness that got her lost on the way.

The song grows louder outside my window . . song of all the rivers flowing into the oceans all over the world . . sung by waves . . by the clouds pushed across the sky like notes sung by small birds.

I watch the trees dancing in the wind . . my reflection like a ghost in the window . . full-grown butterfly wings at my sides . . and I open my mouth to join in . . softly in a whisper . . singing only for myself . . not for any reason except to show that I'm alive.

I know I'll never find the words to ask her all the things I want to . . not today . . maybe not ever . . but maybe I won't have to. Maybe she'll just know everything I want to tell her just by holding my hand.

Maybe all I have to do is be there . . all I have to do is sing the sound of what I feel inside and she'll know. Maybe then she'll understand that the angels never meant to keep me. They always meant to place me in her arms again like a seagull returning a piece of paper that has traveled off the end of the world.

He knocks on the door as he walks in . . his reflection walking toward me with his hands ready to hold mine.

I clear my throat and he tells me he heard me singing. He says it sounded prettier than any songbird could ever sing. His face turns red as he says it and I smile to thank him for saying it because I know how shy it makes him to let me know.

"You ready?" he asks.

I nod real fast. "Ready as I'll ever be, I guess."

Ready to follow the stars to wherever they bring me next. Ready for anything when he holds my hand. I have a family here no matter what else happens. I never have to run away again. I've been born for the last time, maybe because I never need to be afraid to lose love, because love is forever.

And forever is inside me. Forever is always there.

Born Confused	by Tanuja Desai Hidier
Candy	by Kevin Brooks
Cut	by Patricia McCormick
The Dating Diaries	by Kristen Kemp
Fighting Ruben Wolfe	by Markus Zusak
Getting the Girl	by Markus Zusak
Hail Caesar	by Thu-Huong Ha
Heavy Metal and You	by Christopher Krovatin
I Don't Want to Be Crazy	by Samantha Schutz
I Will Survive	by Kristen Kemp
Johnny Hazzard	by Eddie de Oliveira
Kerosene	by Chris Wooding
Kissing the Rain	by Kevin Brooks
Learning the Game	by Kevin Waltman
Lucas	by Kevin Brooks
Lucky	by Eddie de Oliveira
Magic City	by Drew Lerman
Martyn Pig	by Kevin Brooks
Never Mind the Goldbergs	by Matthue Roth
Nowhere Fast	by Kevin Waltman
Perfect World	by Brian James
Pure Sunshine	by Brian James
The Road of the Dead	by Kevin Brooks
Splintering	by Eireann Corrigan
Talking in the Dark	by Billy Merrell
This Is PUSH	by Various Authors
Tyrell	by Coe Booth
Where We Are, What We See	by Various Authors
You Are Here, This Is Now	by Various Authors
You Remind Me of You	by Eireann Corrigan